ISLAND GAMES
MYSTERY OF THE FOUR QUADRANTS

CALEB J. BOYER

DISCARD

ISBN: 978-0-9861036-2-9

Printed in the United States of America

Published By:
Lasting Press
615 NW 2nd Ave #915
Canby, OR 97013
www.LastingPress.com

Cover by: Rory Carruthers Marketing
Project Management and Book Launch by: Rory Carruthers Marketing
www.RoryCarruthers.com

For more information about Caleb J. Boyer or to book him for your next event, book signing, podcast or media interview please visit: www.IslandGamesBook.com

This book was written to inspire others to believe in themselves and to realize that any obstacle can be overcome. I dedicate this book to both of my parents who established my faith in God and taught me the principles of the wizard and the warrior to overcome the challenges of life.

To my mom, Rachael Boyer, for supporting my goal of completing my first book and standing by my side throughout the entire process.

To my dad, Jeff Boyer, for demonstrating to me how hard work and commitment result in success.

ACKNOWLEDGMENTS

There were several important people who made this book a reality, and I would like to personally thank them for their commitment to me and my success in completing this book.

My mom, Rachael Boyer, who pushed me when I didn't want to be pushed and worked with me for countless hours to ensure everything was just right and my imagination continued to soar.

My dad, Jeff Boyer, for inspiring me to recognize that when I believe in myself, I can achieve anything, as any obstacle can be overcome.

My best friend, Quin Peterson, for demonstrating to me what a true friend looks like and for always being by my side through all the challenges in life.

My trainers at the Sanford Power Center, Matthew Taffe and Ryan MacMaster, who taught me perseverance to overcome challenges.

My classmates, friends, and Park Christian School for not only challenging me with tough academic requirements but also helping to guide my character along the way.

CHAPTER

Matthew's body lay limp on the white sandy shore with a cool ocean breeze flowing through his matted, wet hair. He choked on clumps of sand and salty ocean water as he began to awaken. He looked to his right and saw his best friend Ryan lying unconscious further down the shore. He struggled to get his bearings to stand, as he was so weak and dizzy. Pushing hard against the sand on hands and knees, he failed to move and collapsed from the weight of his own body. He just could not find the strength.

As he lay there floating in and out of consciousness, he asked himself, *Where am I? What happened? Where do I belong? I'm so weak and thirsty, I need water. Why don't I remember anything, except my name and Ryan? Ryan! I need to get to Ryan!...*

Matthew lost the battle and fell back into a state of unconsciousness as the scorching sun and salty ocean water continued to beat down against his helpless body.

While Matthew was asleep, he had a vision of him and Ryan. *They were kneeling on the ground in a grassy field. It was a crisp evening; the grass felt so cool and moist. They were surrounded by other kids, but he couldn't see any of their faces. Matthew recalled this moment at football practice when Ryan had just gotten tackled and had the wind knocked out of him. Matthew had come to the rescue, like so many times before.*

The coach, Matthew's dad, was there, but only Matthew could get Ryan to focus and breathe again. Matthew felt a sense of relief when his best friend gasped for air. He remembered them lying on the moist turf for a moment, and he could feel the cool breeze sweeping over his face as he drifted in and out of the vision...

As the sun began to set, Matthew awoke again, this time jolting up as if a lightning bolt had surged through his helpless, limp body. He pushed himself to a sitting position, and noticed Ryan was awake and sitting on the shore staring blankly at the distant ocean horizon.

Although Ryan appeared to be conscious, he was also in a dream state. *Ryan and Matthew were sitting on a couch playing video games. Ryan was destroying Matthew, which was typical since the first time the boys had met and become best friends in kindergarten. Despite the effort Matthew made, Ryan was always the one to walk away with bragging rights. As the boys continued playing, Ryan's mom came in to check on them to see if they needed anything. Ryan knew it was his mom, but he couldn't see her face. Normally, Ryan wouldn't care about looking at his mom, but he felt something different this time and tried so hard to see her face, but Matthew kept distracting him and pulling him back to the game...*

Matthew began to motion and call out to Ryan, but it was useless as Ryan was unaware of his best friend's attempt to connect. Something was keeping Ryan in this trance, and Matthew had to figure out a way to get him back. He knew they were in trouble and needed to find help soon.

Matthew pushed himself onto his hands and knees; his body began to tremble as he slowly crawled over to Ryan. Matthew swiped his hand in front of Ryan's face, but he didn't flinch. He grabbed Ryan by the shoulders and shook him, but it was no use. Ryan seemed to be in his own world; Matthew was scared that if he lost Ryan right now, he would be all alone.

He then did what any best friend would do in this situation. With a stiff backhand, he slapped Ryan in the face to snap him out of his trance. Ryan turned his head sharply and jumped to his feet to defend himself with his arms up over his face and head as if in a boxing stance.

"Ow! What was that for?" Ryan said to Matthew. "Why did you do that to me? Where are we? What's going on?"

"You were in a trance, so I had to slap you to get you out of it. I'm wondering the same thing. I have no idea where we are or how we got here, but what I do know is that we are stranded here, wherever here is, and the sun is setting, so we better figure out what to do or we are dead!" Matthew said as he began to look around.

For the first time since Matthew had opened his eyes after being washed up on the shore, the numbness he felt when he woke was starting to wear off and he was able to focus more clearly on his surroundings. Matthew reached his hand up toward Ryan, who was still standing in his guarded position. Ryan hesitated a bit but then gave Matthew an aggressive tug to pull him to his feet. Ryan flashed a devious smirk at Matthew as if to say, *That's payback for the right hook you gave me, buddy.*

Ryan scanned the island. "The last thing I remember was

sitting in your bean bags at your house playing Playstation; I believe I was royally kicking your butt!"

"Yeah, I remember that too, but it seems like I also remember beating you before too, so don't get too cocky. I'm just not sure how we got from the bean bags to here," Matthew responded with concern in his voice, as he too continued to scan the island for signs of something familiar.

Ryan had a sudden thought and said, "Maybe this is just a dream? Remember that time when I stayed at your house and we ordered pizza, and it was totally greasy, and the next thing I knew I woke up sicker than a dog with food poisoning? I was having really weird dreams then too, so maybe that's what's going on here."

"Based on your reaction from the slap across the face I just gave you, I'm pretty sure you felt that, so this can't be a dream, but let's check again," Matthew declared as he reached over and pinched Ryan's arm.

Ryan felt the pinch and proceeded to fight back by slapping Matthew's arm. Indeed, they were both able to feel the discomfort and knew this had to be a real place, even if they didn't know where they were or how they got there.

"Okay, so we know this can't be a dream, but I can't remember anything else, can you?" Ryan asked in a very concerned tone as he wrestled with that statement thinking back to the vision he had just had while he was waking up on shore. He was sure it had to be his mom, or was it?

Matthew was equally concerned and responded, "No, I just remember you. Although, when I was waking up, I had a memory of my dad coaching us in football, so I know we must have families out there and they must be looking for us."

For now, the memory of each other was the only thing they could rely on. Although both of them were confused, they recognized the importance at this very moment of having each other.

The boys took a few moments to scan the area around them. In the distance beyond the shore, they saw a small, rusty old cargo boat loaded with crates, rocking in the ocean waves. As they turned around, they discovered a huge volcano looming in the distance with a thick jungle separating them from the volcano. It appeared they were on an island as there were no other land areas surrounding them, and even worse…they were indeed alone.

The sun continued to set and the temperature seemed to be dropping at a more rapid rate. Matthew and Ryan were now shivering from head to toe in their wet, sand-covered clothes. They knew they needed to find warmth and shelter fast. Matthew was the first to act and began limping weakly toward the jungle.

Ryan shouted, "Where are you going? We don't know what's in there. What if there are snakes or spiders, or even worse— monsters!"

Matthew responded, "I'm going to get firewood and moss so we can start a fire and at least be covered and warm for the night. This is our only hope to survive. Are you coming or not?"

Ryan grudgingly followed but remained edgy, as he was afraid of what might be lurking in the depths of the jungle. As the boys made their way closer to the jungle, they could hear the swaying of the branches and leaves and the rustling of movement. The sound of the ocean waves was now distant; each of them strangely longed to go back to the spot on the shore where they felt safe.

Ryan stopped suddenly and said, "Matthew, do you think we got kidnapped and the person who kidnapped us brought us to this island? Do you think the kidnapper might still be here?"

"Well, now there's a great thought! Thanks for putting that in my mind right before we get to the edge of the creepy jungle. As if that wasn't enough," Matthew responded with frustration.

Ryan stopped, frustration welling up inside of him too, looked at Matthew and said, "Seriously, we were in your living room and the next thing we know we are on this creepy island all alone. You tell me how we got here then!"

Matthew continued to make his way to the edge of the island. As he did, he responded carefully to Ryan so he didn't make him even more upset, "Ryan, I don't think we got kidnapped because otherwise we would have at least remembered someone coming after us, and if they did kidnap us, why wouldn't they be here now? Besides, we are just two teenage kids, so what could they possibly want with us? I don't know what happened, but all I know is we need to find a way to stay alive for the night so we can try to find a way to signal for help tomorrow."

As they walked cautiously to the edge of the jungle, they both continued to question what happened, how they got onto this island, and why they couldn't remember anything except each other and the brief flashbacks of their parents when waking up on the island. Although they really wanted answers to all those questions, they knew what they really needed to focus on now was the how. How they were going to make it through the night and how they were going to be rescued the next day. They understood that finding warmth and any kind of shelter would be the first thing they needed to survive. Matthew motioned to Ryan to be quiet and follow him, and Ryan obliged.

They reached the edge of the jungle, and it proved to be enough to supply sticks, leaves, and moss. What they didn't find was anything edible to curb the hunger pains they were beginning to recognize in their empty stomachs.

They gathered up as much of the supplies as they could. Filling their arms, they made their way back to the only place they knew, the area they woke up in on the shore. The area they would call home for the night.

As they began to lay the supplies out, Matthew looked at Ryan and asked, "So, do you happen to know how to light this thing?"

Ryan responded, "For some reason, I remember starting a fire once using just sticks like these. Now I remember! It was that one time when you and I went camping with our dads and we lost our matches, so we had to start the fire in the dark with just sticks. It's really the only hope we have right now, so let me give it a try."

Ryan started rubbing two sticks together as fast as he could, and within a few minutes, they had a spark. Ryan and Matthew worked together to kindle the spark, and soon the fire they had started with the moss and branches became the first obstacle they had overcome on the mysterious island.

Once the flames were going strong, they walked back to the jungle to replenish the supplies of sticks and moss, and then they made their way back to the fire. As the boys lay on the barren beach next to the fire and their bodies finally relaxed after the intense day, they began to recognize again the hunger pains that were calling out to them inside their weak bodies. Because they were not able to recall what had happened prior to them arriving on the island, they had no idea how long it had been since they had eaten or had anything to drink. But, the rumbling and nausea were enough to indicate it had been awhile, and they would need to find some source of food and water as soon as the sun came up in the morning.

Matthew rolled over from his back to face the fire and his buddy Ryan. "Do you think we are going to make it through the night?"

Ryan responded, "I don't know, but we have made it this far, so all we can do is pray and get some sleep and see what tomorrow brings."

"Do you remember that huge cargo boat we saw in the ocean just beyond the beach?" Matthew asked.

Ryan said, "Yeah. I do remember seeing that boat, just after you slapped me silly! Do you think we can get to it?"

"I saw a rope going from the beach to the boat. It must be the anchor that is holding it close to shore. Maybe we could swim and pull ourselves along with the rope to get to the boat tomorrow. There are big crates on the boat, so maybe there is food and water and we can use the radio to call for help," Matthew responded.

"That's a good idea," Ryan said. "As soon as the sun comes up, and assuming something hasn't eaten us in the meantime and we don't die of starvation or dehydration, let's go explore the boat first and get off this island as fast as we can."

"I agree. For some reason, I don't have a very good feeling about what this island has to offer us," Matthew said as he started to drift off to sleep.

Ryan rolled onto his back and stared up at the dark sky, wondering if they would live to see another day and actually make it off the island.

"Neither do I, Matthew…neither do I," he said as he drifted off to sleep.

CHAPTER

The sun began to rise. In the distance, there was a piercing sound that startled the boys. Both abruptly awoke from their sleep and jumped to their feet.

"What was that?" Ryan exclaimed as he flung himself around looking for the source of the noise.

"It sounded like a rooster crowing. But why would there be a rooster on an island?"

The rooster crowed again with a loud cock-a-doodle-doo, and this time, the boys weren't afraid; they were hungry and had ideas of capturing the rooster and having a feast for breakfast. However, since the sound was so far off, they didn't think they should be distracted by the rooster. Instead, they decided to stick with their plan of getting to the cargo boat.

Matthew looked at Ryan covered in sand, hair sticking up all over, and clothes torn and tattered from the devastating events of the day before when they washed up on the shore of the island. "You look horrible, dude."

"You aren't so pretty yourself this morning," Ryan responded with frustration. "I can certainly think of better ways to wake up than having to look at you."

Matthew recalled how Ryan was always so careful about how he looked. He had a dark complexion, was already six feet three inches tall, and had dark wavy hair that he let grow out. He was always messing with it to make sure everything was in place and looking good for the girls who seemed to naturally be attracted to him.

Matthew, on the other hand, hadn't quite hit his full height yet and was trailing around six foot tall with blonde hair, fair skin, and lots of freckles, which made him always appear younger. He kept his hair short and didn't care to deal with combing it unless he absolutely had to or his mom got on him to clean himself up. Matthew was more interested in hanging out with his best friend Ryan than about caring what the girls liked or didn't like.

As Matthew reflected on what they normally looked like compared to what he was seeing now as he looked at Ryan, he became very concerned about getting the help they needed to be rescued from the island.

"We better do something fast to get some food and water before we lose all of our strength and our chance to survive," Matthew said.

Ryan looked off across the ocean and saw that the rusty old cargo boat was still where it was the day before. He looked back at Matthew and said, "Now is our chance to do something about this. The wind is calm and the tide is low, so that means…let's go!"

As they both ran toward the edge of the beach, they stripped off their shirts and ran into the ocean water. The boys gasped with the shock of the cold water pressing against their chests, but they had no choice but to proceed with the plan to get to the cargo boat.

"Grab the rope!" Ryan shouted to Matthew, who was ahead of him in the water.

Matthew reached out ahead of himself as he took another stroke swimming toward the rope and grabbed on to it to pull himself forward.

"I've got it!" Matthew exclaimed with excitement.

Matthew swung the rope toward Ryan. He grabbed on to it and pulled himself up just behind Matthew. Both boys pulled and swam their way along the rope in the frigid water. After what seemed to be a lifetime, they finally reached the platform of the cargo boat.

With extreme exhaustion, Matthew pulled himself up, steadied himself on the edge of the platform, and reached his hand down to the ocean water to pull his friend to safety. Just as Matthew was about to grasp Ryan's hand, he noticed a swirling in the water, and a giant fin came to the surface.

"It's a shark! Get out of the water! Get out of the water!" Matthew shouted as Ryan scrambled to grasp Matthew's cold, wet, trembling hand.

Ryan frantically locked hand-in-hand with Matthew, and they both pulled as hard as they could to get Ryan to safety. Ryan flung his right leg onto the platform of the cargo boat. Just as he began to lift his left leg, the shark lurched forward and snagged the bottom of his left pant leg, ripping it to shreds and pulling Ryan back down into the water.

Ryan screamed desperately as he kicked and landed a sharp blow to the shark's nose. His pant leg was still intertwined in the shark's teeth. As the shark pulled away, he made the final rip and Ryan's pants became the shark's breakfast. Ryan frantically swam back to the platform where Matthew was standing and shaking from head to toe, screaming again for Ryan's hand to pull him back onto the platform.

Ryan reached up, grabbed Matthew's hand, and this time, Matthew was able to pull Ryan to the safety of the platform. They looked out just beyond the boat and saw the giant fin coming back toward them. They scrambled to the ladder and climbed the rusty rungs as the shark took the final lunge onto the platform.

His mouth was inches away from Ryan's feet and the weight of the shark's body could be felt as it pressed against the platform and rocked the boat. The boys managed to climb further up the ladder when suddenly the bottom rung broke and Ryan's foot slipped down toward the shark's large, sharp teeth.

This time, Matthew took matters into his own hands and reached down and grabbed Ryan's arm and yanked him up onto the surface of the cargo boat. The shark slipped back into the water, but it continued to swirl around the platform as if waiting for the "breakfast that got away" to be served again. Matthew and Ryan lay on the hard surface of the deck gasping for air, exhausted from the struggle they had just been through, hoping that was the end of this awful nightmare and they would be rescued once they could radio for help.

As they lay there, Ryan turned weakly toward Matthew and said, "Thanks, man. I couldn't have made it without you. Although the shark ate my pants, I'm sure glad it was my pants and not me that was his breakfast!"

"You're welcome. Now let's get going and see if we can find you some pants and better yet, some supplies and a way off this boat and this island," Matthew responded.

Matthew rose to his feet and Ryan followed. The boys began to explore the deck of the boat. Along the sides of the boat deck there were crates stacked two high, and just beyond the crates at the front of the boat was the bridge.

"Should we start with the crates or go to the bridge first?" Ryan asked Matthew.

"Let's start with the crates because we need some supplies and food fast. I'm just praying we will find something in these things that we can salvage, especially some pants for you because I sure don't want to have to look at you running around in your underwear!" Matthew said as he moved toward the closest crate.

The boys looked at all sides of the crates and realized there was no distinct opening. They were made of wood and had overlapping boards crisscrossed along all sides of the box. Matthew made the decision to kick the side of the first crate in. With ease from the first kick, the crate imploded and coated the inside of the box with, unfortunately, nothing but dust. There were no supplies. The crate was completely empty and useless.

They each took turns kicking the crates and repeated this process several more times, but they became extremely discouraged at their inability to source some supplies. A hopeless sense of dread began to overwhelm the boys. On the final crate, both boys kicked in the side of the box, but this time, they kicked together at the same time.

This time, supplies began to burst from the depths of the crate. The boys screamed, jumped up and down, and began to scoop up the supplies into their arms. It appeared the teamwork paid off again this time.

They filtered through the supplies that poured out of the box and discovered a knife, packets of food, bottles of water, two small cups, a rope, matches, clothes and shoes, a watch, two blankets, two backpacks, and a small wooden box with a keyhole, but no key.

Matthew looked at Ryan and said, "This is starting to get creepy. It's as if someone placed these supplies here specifically for us. Obviously, they planted us here too. I bet they are watching us right now!" Matthew could not help but wonder who would play this kind of joke on someone.

Ryan responded, "Yeah. I bet they planned the shark attack to test us. Now I'm really upset because I lost my pants over that one. Even worse, it could have been my leg!"

"Regardless of who or what might be behind this," Matthew chimed in, "we still need to figure out how to get the heck off this boat and this island."

Although the boys were relieved by the discovery of the supplies, their focus quickly shifted to communicating for help. Ryan began to move toward the bridge and motioned for Matthew to follow. The boys entered the bridge and immediately saw that their hope for communication was ruined as all the controls on the cargo boat were torn apart and damaged beyond repair.

Ryan leaned against the ship's wall and slid down until he thumped onto the floor of the bridge. He sat there with nothing on, other than his underwear, and he held his head in his hands, shaking his head back and forth. He began to tremble with fear and exhaustion.

"What now?" Ryan asked weakly, as Matthew continued to scurry around the bridge hoping desperately to find something he could salvage to communicate with the outside world.

Matthew finally came to a stop and stared blankly out the ship's window to the ocean beyond and responded, "I think it's time we get something to eat and drink. We are both exhausted and starving. If we don't get something now, I'm afraid we won't last much longer out here. Besides, I don't know what else to do right now; I just can't think anymore."

Ryan lifted his head from his trembling hands, nodded in agreement, and Matthew helped Ryan to his feet. The boys walked with shoulders slumped and heads hung low back to the cargo deck where they had left the supplies. They plopped themselves down next to the supplies, leaned against the broken crate, and began to sort the food and water to ration what they had.

Each took one packet of food and a bottle of water and slowly ate and drank. They could feel the strength beginning to return to their bodies as the food made its way down into their empty stomachs. The food was thick, like some kind of paste, but it actually tasted like meat. Once the food hit the pit of their stomachs, the aftertaste finally began to set in and the boys recognized it was the worse tasting meal they had ever eaten, but quickly became the most appreciated meal of their lives.

The boys savored the food packets and fresh water and reflected on the events of the day. They realized their plan to get to the cargo boat had taken up most of the day and a lot of extra energy they hadn't anticipated. They would definitely need to try to conserve their energy going forward as they did not know what their source of food would be after the food packets and water were gone.

Although they were happy they were able to acquire some essential supplies, with no radio communication option from the bridge of the cargo boat they knew a different plan would be required to communicate with anyone who might be trying to rescue them. They had originally planned to be rescued from the boat and didn't think about having to get back to shore. Now, they not only had to find a way to get back to shore with their supplies, they had to find a way to get off the island without radio communication.

As the sun was beginning to set on another long day, the boys knew they would not have enough time or energy to swim back to shore, so they decided to sleep on the boat for the night. After finishing their food packets and drinking the last few drops of water, they began to pack the supplies into the backpacks. Matthew took the knife and the small wooden box, wrapped the watch around his wrist, and then Ryan grabbed the matches and the rope. They split the food, water, and cups evenly and then changed into the jeans, t-shirts, and shoes, and each grabbed a blanket.

After the supplies were split, Ryan crawled into the crate and motioned Matthew toward him and said, "Let's sleep inside the crate tonight because it will at least be warm and will shelter us through the night."

"Good idea, Ryan," Matthew said as he gathered his backpack and blanket and made his way into the crate next to his best friend.

As they lay there inside the crate on the deck of the cargo

boat, Matthew said to Ryan, "Why do you think they put us here?"

Ryan yawned and responded, "What I'm really wondering is who 'they' are, and what else 'they' have planned for us, because none of this has been very fun so far. Nothing makes sense to me right now. Why did 'they' choose us? Why can't we remember anything about our lives? I still can't remember anything clearly."

"Maybe it's a test to see how strong we are; it's a reality TV show, we just can't see the cameras, and maybe we will win a big prize when it's all done. And, if that's the case, all I have to say is…'Hello, world! You can't break us! Let the games begin!'" Matthew shouted loudly as his voice echoed through the crate.

Both boys shifted around inside the crate and made themselves as comfortable as they could despite their circumstances. They covered themselves with their blankets and used their stuffed backpacks as makeshift pillows.

Ryan stretched and said, "I don't know about you, but fighting off a shark, swimming for my life, and now lying inside this hard crate, I'm pretty sure I'm going to be sore and miserable in the morning."

"Yep, I hear you, man," Matthew responded as he rolled over onto his side and watched as the last sliver of light left the opening of the crate as the sun set in the distance.

The cargo boat gently rocked in the ocean waves and lulled the boys off to sleep. Little did they know, the games had just begun…

CHAPTER

The sun began to rise and the rays of light peeked through the cracks of the dusty old crate. Off in the distance, the sound of a cock-a-doodle-doo echoed from across the shore and was enough to startle Matthew from his sleep. He shifted uncomfortably and raised himself to a sitting position with a groan and a loud moan that caused Ryan to wake.

"I just heard that rooster crow again," Matthew said. "I'm thinking this rooster is going to be our new alarm clock. I think we should name it. I have a list of three names already; what do you think about Jorge, Donald, or Reggie?"

Ryan sat up and scowled at Matthew and with a slight edge in his voice said, "Are you serious, dude? We just spent the night on an old, rusted, abandoned boat, in a crate, on a hard wooden floor, trying to escape a deserted island, and all you can think about is naming a dumb rooster?"

"Ummmmm...yeah, that's what I was thinking about," Matthew responded in a friendly bantering manner, and went on to say, "I've got to keep my mind on something other than waking up next to you the way you look this morning."

"Okay already. Reggie it is. Maybe Reggie will bring us some good luck, and I think we are due for some good—" Ryan stated before he was abruptly cut off by the sound of a loud CRACK!

Matthew crawled quickly out of the crate and Ryan followed. They gathered their blankets and backpacks, and as they got to their feet, they could feel the boat shuttering and shifting, rocking deeply to one side and then the other. They could immediately feel the adrenaline start to build again inside their veins as they recognized the danger that was coming.

They scurried to pack their blankets into their backpacks, and just as they stuffed them in and zipped up the backpacks, the boat started to descend quickly into the ocean. They knew they were headed for another unexpected cold ocean bath.

They quickly put their backpacks onto their backs. Matthew shouted to Ryan as he motioned for Ryan to follow him to the edge of the boat, "Come on! Hurry up! Let's go! This boat is going down and we need to get off this thing fast!"

Both boys stepped back to take a running start to jump off the boat. Just as they did, the back half of the boat broke off and separated from the front half where the boys were standing. They could feel the boat taking a nosedive and the cold water starting to rise onto their feet. As they struggled to maintain their balance, they stepped back again and took their running start. This time, they jumped into the frigid, blue ocean water.

Luckily, their backpacks helped them stay afloat as the waves quickly whipped up and beat relentlessly against their bodies on their initial plunge into the ocean. This time, there was no rope to help pull them back to shore, and they were stuck further out from shore than they had realized when they made the original swim out to the cargo boat. In the distance, they could see the volcano and the outline of the shore that looked very inviting as the water was so cold.

The boys started to swim in the direction of the shore and struggled to overcome the waves that felt like tendrils pulling them down into the depths of the ocean with each stroke they took. They continued to press on but realized this was going to take a while.

Breathing heavily, Matthew looked at Ryan and said, "We need to pace ourselves because I can't fight these waves for long without taking a break."

Ryan agreed by slowing down and coming to a float. The boys floated for a few moments and then Ryan suddenly grabbed Matthew's backpack and said frantically, "Remember the shark that almost ate me for breakfast? What if he comes back? What if we can't make it to shore? What if—"

Matthew cut Ryan off and said, "Dude, stop! You are going to hyperventilate, and then we will be in big trouble. We need to focus on working together, just like we did getting to the boat, fighting off the shark, and when we kicked the crate together and found the supplies. We have to do this together, so stay calm and let's pace ourselves so we don't drown."

Ryan took a deep breath and said, "Okay, but let's get going now because just the thought of that shark is enough to get me back to shore."

The boys continued to swim, and then rest, and repeated the process over and over. They didn't recall the swim out to the cargo boat being as diffcult, and they felt like they were in a losing battle as each wave crashed against them. They could feel the fatigue increase as they swam. They were moving their arms and legs, but after what felt like hours in the water, they could not feel anything. It was simply a motion that became programmed in their brains as if they were robots that had no control.

They paused for another breath. As they floated helplessly in the water, Matthew looked at Ryan and saw the fear in his eyes, as he recognized Ryan was struggling to keep his head above water. Matthew grabbed Ryan's backpack and began to pull him along when suddenly he looked ahead and realized they were less than 50 yards away from the shore!

Matthew pulled harder on Ryan's backpack and shouted, "Ryan! We are close! You can do it, buddy! Keep swimming!" With their last ounce of energy, both boys stretched their arms out in front of them, kicked their legs as hard as they could, and finally felt the sand and rocks of the beach as they slid their bellies onto the shore. They crawled, on hands and knees, a few more feet out of the cold water and collapsed with exhaustion. Both boys were too tired to carry on, and the sand felt warm and inviting as it pressed against their cold bodies.

Without moving, Ryan said to Matthew, "Thank you for saving my life again."

"We did it together," Matthew responded weakly.

The boys lay on the shore for what seemed like ages as they drifted in and out of consciousness. While they lay there, they each had visions of scary experiences in places they had never been and never wanted to go. Each time they would wake, the soft warm sand would invite them back to sleep, and each time they would travel to a different location with a different challenge they would have to face.

Over the course of a few hours, the sun continued to scorch their bodies and dried their sopping, wet clothes. Matthew finally began to wake and made the first move as he sat up and looked off into the distance where the cargo boat once was and saw nothing but open water. No boat, no rescue ships, nobody on their way to save them from this horrible nightmare. He reached over and tapped Ryan on the shoulder and nudged him to wake up.

Ryan looked up, with his arm over his eyes blocking the rays of the brilliant sun, and said, "Mommy...I don't want to go to school today. Leave me alone, I just want to sleep longer...ugh!"

Matthew was shocked by his friend's words. He reached into his backpack and grabbed his cup and crawled over to the edge of the shore and scooped up some cold, salty, ocean water and tossed it onto Ryan's face. Ryan sat up quickly and spit out the water that had gotten into his mouth directly back onto Matthew's face. Both boys were once again offcially awake.

"Seriously, man. Was that necessary?" Ryan asked Matthew as he continued to wipe the water off his face trying to keep it from getting into his eyes.

"You were calling me Mommy! Yeah, I would say it certainly was necessary. You were getting kind of creepy on me, so I had to do something. Were you dreaming?" Matthew asked.

Ryan hesitated and then responded, "I was having strange visions of really awful places with beasts chasing us. You were there...or maybe you were the beast? I can't remember, but then all of a sudden, I was lying in my bed at home with the smell of bacon and eggs floating in the air. I think my mom was just about to deliver me a gourmet breakfast in bed. Then my worst nightmare happened again when I woke up and saw you!" Even though he didn't see her in the dream, he longed to be back home with his mom again instead of on this stupid island. He was exhausted and frustrated, and just wanted to go home.

"Well, my worst nightmare actually did happen. We both must have fallen asleep when we got back to shore. I had a terrible nightmare about being in the jungle, and you were hanging on the edge of a cliff. You started to slip and couldn't hang on anymore. I tried to grab you, but then I slipped off too, and when I slipped, I woke up. Now that was a nightmare!" Matthew said as he continued to brush the sand off his clothes and body.

"Wow! That sounds scary. Maybe we could just go back to the nice breakfast in bed," Ryan responded as he stood up and started to take a look around the island once again.

Matthew stood and said, "Well, the good news is that we made it back to shore. It looks like we have some time before the sun will set again. At least we are safe for now, but we should probably be thinking about getting supplies and figure out another strategy to get us off this island."

"At least tonight we will have blankets to use instead of moss. Maybe we should lay out our stuff from our backpacks and let things dry out while we go get some more wood for tonight," Ryan said as he started to unzip his backpack and lay out his supplies.

As Matthew followed along, the boys realized their backpacks must have been virtually waterproof as nothing seemed to be wet or ruined despite the many hours in the ocean. Each of the boys gathered their new belongings and headed up the shore closer to the edge of the jungle where they had made the fire the first night they woke up on the mystery island. They laid their stuff down again, felt the hunger pains return, and realized they hadn't had anything to eat or drink since the night before.

Matthew opened his backpack and found his packet of food and a bottle of water. He recognized there were only a few more bottles of fresh water; this would not allow them to survive long without finding another water source.

"We are going to need to find some fresh water. I think we should go explore the jungle tomorrow to see if we can find some more food and water, and better yet, a way off this creepy island," Matthew said as he sat down and then took a bite of his food and gulped down some water.

Ryan did the same and said, "I agree, but I'm scared…Mommy!" He said with a smile on his face as he grinned from ear to ear and then stuck his tongue out at Matthew.

"You're sick and demented; you obviously need some help. So, we definitely need to get off this island fast to get you some help for sure," Matthew responded as he turned away and looked back toward the jungle, wondering what lurked inside its depths.

Matthew wondered if his visions were foreshadowing events to come. Who would do this to them? Did they put those visions in his head? Were they trying to communicate something to him? These past few days were the worst days of his life, at least what he could remember and imagine, and yet, he had a strange sense that this adventure was not over yet.

He continued to think about the need to get off the horrible island and yet, the fear set in about all the what-ifs that might happen if they moved from the safe place they were currently in.

At least here, someone might be able to see them if they were trying to find them and rescue them. He was sure that their parents or someone out there must be looking for him and Ryan.

As he finished the last bites of his food packet and indulged in the last drops of his water, the events of the past few days continued to race through his mind, and images of what was within the depths of the jungle became more vivid.

He looked over at Ryan, who seemed to be entranced in his own world. Matthew consciously stopped thinking and began hoping his imagination was worse than what was actually behind the jungle curtain.

CHAPTER

The boys finished off their rationed food and headed toward the edge of the jungle to repeat the process from the first night on the island. They gathered some more wood, sticks, branches, and dried up leaves and each carried a few loads to the campsite. As they made their way back to the campfire on their second trip, Matthew suddenly stopped dead in his tracks.

"Hey! I think I see a light out there on the ocean. Do you see that, Ryan?" Matthew said as he dropped his sticks and started to run toward the shore.

"Wait up!" Ryan hollered as he followed in the tracks of his best friend.

Matthew was frantically waving his arms in the direction of the light and then stopped and turned around and motioned for Ryan to go back and start a fire in the hopes that the fire or smoke would cause someone to notice they were on the island.

"Ryan, go start the fire; I will go get some more sticks to build out S.O.S. in case someone is trying to send help to find us. They might be able to see the smoke and fire and maybe even see the S.O.S. on the shore," Matthew said as he ran back toward the edge of the jungle to get some more sticks.

Ryan started on the fire and this time found it to be much easier since he was able to use one of the matches from his supplies to get the fire started quickly. Before long, the fire was burning and the flames were shooting high into the dusky night sky. Matthew was working frantically on the S.O.S. letters when he looked up and saw the light he had noticed before had suddenly disappeared into the night.

He stopped where he was and sat down, cradling his head in his hands, exhausted from another long day and the extensive effort they had made with no hope of someone rescuing them. He knew they would certainly be spending another night on the horrible island. As he sat there, he looked up to confirm that the light was indeed gone. Ryan saw Matthew sitting and went over and sat next to him.

This time, Ryan had to comfort Matthew and said, "Don't worry. We know there might actually be people out there looking for us, and I'm sure they will come back. We will get off this island one way or another. Besides, at least we have each other because it sure would be hard if we had to do this alone. Right?"

Matthew looked up at his best friend, whose hair was standing straight up and messed up all over, covered in sand from head to toe, eyes red and swollen, and said, "I wouldn't want to be any other place than with you on this five-star vacation resort island!"

He put his arm around his friend's shoulders, and they laughed for the first time since they found themselves on the mystery island. They stood up and finished the S.O.S. letters together and then went back to the fire Ryan had built to refresh the wood and keep it burning in hopes of someone still out there looking for them.

The boys realized that while they were working on the S.O.S. letters and sending smoke signals from the fire, the sun had completely set and the moon was rising in the distant sky. They sat down by the fire and looked up at the night sky and saw a shooting star.

"Look! Did you see that shooting star? We should make a wish," Ryan exclaimed as he pointed in the direction of the shooting star.

"Yeah. I saw it," Matthew said and continued on to claim his wish, "I wish that we would get off this island. Don't you?"

"Yeah. I wish we could get off this island quickly too, but if we can't, I wish I had a hot girlfriend here with me instead of you!" Ryan said as he dodged the right fist of Matthew that was suddenly coming toward his face as a result of the comment Ryan had just made.

Matthew responded with his own bit of sarcasm, "I'm way prettier than any girl you could ever get. Maybe tomorrow you can find a beast in the jungle who will claim you as her boyfriend."

"Ha! Ha! Very funny. Let's see how you react when you come face to face with my 'girlfriend' tomorrow. I bet you will pee your pants, you're such a wimp," Ryan responded with another huge grin on his face.

"Okay, okay. Let's get back to business here and figure out what we are going to do to get through the night and survive tomorrow in the jungle while we scavenge for food and fresh water," Matthew said as he tossed another branch in the fire.

Ryan then came up with what he thought was an excellent strategy and said, "I think as soon as Reggie crows, we should head into the part of the jungle closest to the water. That way if something goes wrong or we get a bad feeling about something, we can run back out here to the shore. Maybe there might be fresh water in a stream flowing into the ocean and fruit trees near the stream."

"I think that's a good idea. You should take the knife and go in first in case your 'girlfriend' is there to greet us. Or, you might just want to pick some flowers for her along that stream next to the fruit trees." Matthew said as he dodged the vicious right hook of Ryan.

After the long bantering back and forth, the boys decided to have their last packet of food and bottle of water for the night. They called it the last supper and prayed that tomorrow would bring them some opportunity for real food. They each had two more packets of food and two more bottles of water, but they had no idea what tomorrow would bring, and they knew they needed to ration even more than before.

They packed their supplies back into their backpacks and laid out their blankets next to the fire. As they sat there staring at the fire dancing in front of them, Matthew felt like he had forgotten something, but what could it be? He traced his steps back to the jungle, back to the S.O.S. words, and back to washing up on the shore, but nothing clicked in his memory. Until suddenly, he thought back to the cargo boat and realized it was the small wooden box. He had left it outside the crate the night before on the boat because he didn't want to lay on it in his backpack that he had used as a pillow.

"Ryan, I forgot that small wooden box on the boat. I didn't pack it because I didn't want to have to sleep on it and now it's gone. What if it had something important in it? Obviously, whoever planted us here and planted the supplies had a plan for that box, and now it's gone forever!" Matthew said as he started to get to his feet to walk toward the shore. "Maybe I should go see if it washed up on the shore?"

"Get real! It's pitch black, we have no lights, and there is no way you are going to find it now. Who knows if there was anything in it, and besides, there was no key anyway, so we couldn't even open it without cracking it open, even if it was here. Now lie down and let's try to get some sleep. We are going to have another long day trying to figure out how to get ourselves out of here," Ryan said as he lay down and adjusted his backpack under his head.

"You're right," Matthew said as he made his way back to his blanket and did the same as Ryan.

Matthew adjusted his backpack and rolled onto his side to face the fire. He could already feel the sleep setting in. The boys felt the warmth of the fire and for the first time in two days, they felt relaxed. The fire crackling, the ocean waves crashing against the shore, and the stars sparkling above them were enough to lull the boys into a sleepy trance...

As the boys drifted in and out of their sleepy trance, they each had visions of entering the jungle and having some kind of green gas overtake them as they were trying to escape. Suddenly, the boys awoke in a white room. They were now sitting up on two beds that were positioned in the center of the room. There was nothing around them other than a cold sterile floor. Directly in front of them was a door with a reflective glass window. The boys sat there and stared blankly at each other. Were they dreaming? Had they been rescued? Or, was this a trap?

Ryan jumped out of his bed and just about collapsed as his feet hit the cold floor. He hadn't expected to still be woozy from whatever that was that gassed them out in the jungle. It was all so confusing now. Were they really in a jungle or were they in what appeared to be a lab environment all along and they were dreaming about being washed up on the shore of the mysterious island?

As Ryan regained his footing, he motioned for Matthew to join him. Without saying a word, they both knew something didn't feel right about this. They tried to open the door, but it was locked. They attempted to peer out the window down the corridor, but just as they were scanning the area outside their white room, the room began to fill with green fog and within a split second they had passed out…

Matthew and Ryan woke suddenly from their sleepy trance as a loud growl arose from the inner part of the island. Both boys shot awake and jumped to their feet. The boys looked around but could not figure out where the noise was coming from.

"Where did that noise come from? Where did it go? Get out the knife in case it comes this way," Ryan whispered frantically as he looked around the island and as far into the jungle as he could see in the pitch black to try to determine where the noise was coming from.

They remained as quiet as they could in hopes that they would not attract attention to themselves as Matthew dug desperately through his backpack to try and find the knife. His hands were shaking and he could hardly even unzip the backpack, let alone find the small knife buried in its depths.

This became a big lesson as he realized he needed to keep the knife on him at all times. He continued to dig and finally felt the small wooden handle. He ripped it out of the backpack and waved it aggressively around in the night air, nearly slicing a piece of Ryan's hand in the process!

"Hey, dude! Watch where you are swinging that thing!" Ryan whispered angrily at Matthew as he ducked out of the way of Matthew's flailing arms. "Maybe I should be the one to carry that as you obviously aren't certified and safety trained to handle that big weapon."

"Well, maybe that was your 'girlfriend' calling out to you because she can't wait until tomorrow. So, maybe you should take the knife and go get her now," Matthew said sarcastically as he stopped for a moment to catch his breath after waking suddenly from his sleepy trance.

Ryan continued to look around and finally said softly, "Seriously, you need to keep that thing on you at all times. We can't wait for you to be digging it out. There's got to be more of those, whatever that was, inside that jungle. I don't want to come face to face with one of those 'things' without the little protection we have. Better yet, I think we should start thinking about making our own weapons as that tiny knife will likely only take out a squirrel at best."

"Yeah, yeah! I hear you. At least I found it. I'm more worried right now about shutting up so we can hear if it growls again in order to see where it is coming from," Matthew said as he sat down on his blanket next to the fire and continued to scan around the island, waiting for the sound to repeat itself but hoping it would not.

After waiting several minutes and hearing nothing, Matthew said, "Do you think we should each take turns staying awake in case that thing comes after us?"

"Yeah, I vote for you to stay up all night and for me to sleep here next to the fire on my comfy new blanket," Ryan declared sarcastically.

"Your humor is not impressing me right now," Matthew responded as he continued to scan the island.

Ryan gave his best friend his typical sarcastic look while flipping his lower lip down and executing the most dramatic pouty face he could and said, "You are going to make me cry. I'm just trying to make simple suggestions. I'm confident that the way you were waving that knife around that I am in good hands if the beast attempts to attack!"

Ryan sat down for a few moments and then could not help but lie back down as he was so tired and the fatigue had won over the fear of being eaten by an unknown beast. Matthew followed along after making a few more scans across the island.

"Whatever!" Matthew said as he lay down on his back, stabbed the knife into the sand next to him, and continued to hold the handle just in case he needed to grab it quickly again. "Let's both just get some sleep so we can try to get the heck out of here tomorrow," Matthew said as he adjusted his blanket on the sand.

As they lay there, Matthew turned to Ryan and started to describe the dream he had when they had both drifted off earlier. Ryan sat up, stunned by what Matthew was describing since he had the exact dream. Neither one of them knew how to put this together and started to question whether they were really living this nightmare or if they were actually trapped somewhere else and dreaming about being on the island. Exhaustion had set in, and the only thing they knew to do at this point was to get some rest and see where they ended up tomorrow.

Before long, Matthew's hand, which had been gripping his knife in the sand, slipped off the handle, and he and Ryan both drifted off to sleep.

CHAPTER

Cock-a-doodle-doo! Reggie crowed, and the boys responded by slowly lifting their heads off their backpacks, rubbing their eyes, and pushing themselves up to a sitting position. They were now familiar with their morning alarm, and after another long day and night, they didn't feel the need to move too quickly this morning.

Despite the late-night scare from the growling within the depths of the jungle and the strange dreams, the boys managed to sleep off and on while occasionally stirring from the noises that continued throughout the night. Although the boys wanted to sleep longer, they knew they couldn't because they had to go into the jungle today. They recognized that since they had actually woken up on the island, their vision of being in the lab must have only been another trick on their brains last night while they were sleeping. Now, entering the jungle was their only hope to see if they could get themselves out of this mysterious nightmare.

Unfortunately, Ryan woke up on the wrong side of the blanket. "Seriously, Reggie! You had to wake us up! Can't we sleep for five more minutes? Ugh!" Ryan said as he ran his hands through his messed up, sand-filled hair.

"Get used to it, Ryan. That's one mystery we don't need to solve. Reggie is going to crow every morning. In fact, I think it's a good thing; otherwise, you would be sleeping all day and we wouldn't get anything done. So, deal with it. Better yet, if you can't handle waking up to the beautiful sound of Reggie, I will personally pick you up, before Reggie crows, and throw you in the ocean for a nice refreshing morning dip," Matthew said with a little morning sarcasm.

"Fine. I'll get up without complaining, but maybe when we go into the jungle today, we can get some coffee beans so we can make coffee in the morning. That would really cheer me up so I wouldn't have to be so cranky every morning," Ryan said as he continued to complain to Matthew.

"Yeah. While you are picking your flowers for your 'girlfriend,' why don't you add coffee beans to the shopping list?" Matthew responded and then continued on to say, "Let's eat and get going. We have no idea what to expect today, and we need to take advantage of all the daylight we can."

Ryan finally settled down, and both boys pulled out their food packets and started to eat. As they were devouring their food and drinking their water, they realized that after this meal, they would be down to their last packet of food and last bottle of water, so they would only have one more "meal."

They had forgotten they were running low on both essentials. They slowed down to savor the last few bites and then carefully started to pack the remaining food and water back into their backpacks.

"Now we really need to find food and water or else we are as good as dead," Ryan said as he looked at the last supplies in his backpack. He started daydreaming about fruit and a nice little stream when Matthew snapped his fingers and shook him from his dream.

"Ryan, seriously! Snap out of it, dude. We have wasted enough time. We need to pack up and get going because I'm sure we have another long day ahead of us. Hopefully, we will find some food and water today, but if we don't, we are going to have to look tomorrow, assuming we are still alive and not serving as your 'girlfriend's' lunch!" Matthew said as he got up and finished packing his supplies into his backpack.

Matthew grabbed his backpack and started walking toward the jungle, leaving Ryan behind. He didn't know what to expect as he moved closer to the edge of the jungle, but he wasn't about to hang around watching Ryan pout about not having all of his needs met for the day. Ryan began to chase after him, but Matthew didn't slow down and didn't look back.

"Wait up! Wait for me! You can't just leave without me!" Ryan said as he scrambled to get his stuff together so he could catch up to Matthew, who was now reaching the edge of the jungle.

Matthew was standing at the edge of the jungle when Ryan finally caught up to him. Matthew was staring blankly into the thick branches of the jungle as if he was trying to look through it with x-ray vision. Ryan waved his hand in front of Matthew's eyes to break his trance, but he remained focused.

"I know what we really need right now," Ryan said as he started digging in his pockets as if he was pulling out an imaginary item. "An iPod!"

That was enough to break Matthew out of his trance. He looked back at Ryan with confusion and exclaimed, "An iPod? Are you kidding me? Ugh! I'm about ready to request a new partner in this deal."

"Yeah! An iPod so we can play Guns N' Roses—'Welcome to the Jungle!'" Ryan said as he dropped to his knee and started playing air guitar as he sang wildly while tossing his head around. "Welcome to the jungle, we've got fun and games..." He stopped suddenly and said, "Oh, that's all I can remember."

"Well thank God for that!" Matthew said as he turned back around to continue working on his strategy for entering the jungle. "I was about to pull my knife back out because I thought the beast might have overtaken you in the night, the way you are acting this morning."

Ryan rose to his feet and raised his imaginary guitar over his head and brought it down rapidly as if he was smashing his guitar on the sandy shore and said, "Just trying to lighten things up a bit before we enter the unknown, but now I have said goodbye forever to my precious guitar."

"While you say your last goodbyes to your guitar, I've got a plan; I'm going to go in. If you choose to join me, try to keep up because I'm not going to be babysitting you along the way," Matthew said as he took his knife out of his backpack and took his first step into the jungle.

Ryan quickly followed behind his best friend, as he certainly did not want to be left alone. Although their friendship was strong, it was becoming even more crucial for the boys to remain closer than they had ever been. The challenges of the past few days and nights had caused the two to grow weary of each other, but Ryan realized they would be nowhere without one another. And he certainly wouldn't be alive right now without his buddy saving his life several times over the past few days.

As he continued to keep pace with Matthew, he thought about how thankful he was for their friendship and trust in each other. He had always been the goofy one and Matthew the practical one, and it was proving to be a perfect combination on this journey they were on. He knew that regardless of what happened and how different they were at times, the two of them together could overcome any obstacle. He also knew that when they were sarcastic toward one another, it was all in fun and neither of them would be offended. That's why their friendship was so strong. Since the time they met in kindergarten, they had become more like brothers than simply best friends.

Ryan was proud of the way he and Matthew had already overcome some life-threatening challenges while on the island, and he knew the experience had already changed who they were and what their friendship meant to one another. The reflection of the past few days and the strength he found in his friend seemed to light an internal spark of energy. He used that renewed sense of energy to remain focused on the task at hand to conquer the nasty jungle.

As they slowly made their way through the edge of the jungle, the vines and leaves continued to get thicker and the bugs were starting to multiply. They continued to sweep the vines, leaves, and bugs away from their faces and before long, their arms were growing tired and their hands were raw from the small scrapes and cuts they accumulated along the way.

The inner part of the jungle remained dense. The

temperature was starting to become a bit cooler with the shade, but more humid. The bugs were starting to subside; however, the boys could hear the noise of animals calling out and echoing through the jungle.

"Shhhhh," Matthew whispered to Ryan as he held his finger in front of his mouth signaling for Ryan to stop and listen. "I think I hear something. It sounds like running water. I think it's coming from over there," Matthew said as he pointed in the direction of a thick set of vines.

"Yeah, I hear it too," Ryan whispered back as the boys started to make their way through the thick jungle floor toward the area where they had heard the sound.

Each step they took became more challenging as they fought the thick brush, and their legs began to feel as if they had cement filling their shoes. Several hours had already passed since they entered the jungle, and by this time, they were sweating and once again feeling exhaustion set in. They felt like they would never make it to what they thought might be the stream they had heard and maybe the source of the fresh water they desperately needed.

"Ugh! Let's take a break," Matthew said as he stopped moving and found a fallen tree that had started to rot on the jungle floor. He sat down and motioned for Ryan to join him. "But I hear it. It's close now, I know it," Ryan said as he tried to pull Matthew up off the log.

"We've heard it for a long time now, but it sure doesn't feel like we are getting any closer," Matthew said as he looked down at the watch he found in the supplies from the crate on the boat.

The watch was still ticking despite the fact that the face had cracked along the side. The watch remained a constant reminder that time was dwindling away quickly and the boys had not made much progress. They were now too far into the jungle to turn back to the security of the beach they had for the past few days, but they needed to get to the stream so they could get some fresh water and try to find shelter for another long night ahead.

After sitting for a while, Matthew felt rested enough to press on. He rose to his feet and said, "Okay, I think you might be right, Ryan. Maybe it is closer. Let's keep walking so we can get there before it gets dark, which I'm thinking will happen quicker inside the jungle with all these trees blocking out the sun."

"It's about time you listen to me for once. Let me take the lead this time and you can be the one to be hit by all the swinging branches as I plow through it ahead of you," Ryan said with his devious smile.

Matthew motioned for him to move on and said, "Whatever! Let's get going."

The boys continued to make their way toward the sound of the running water. With each step, they visualized the opportunity that lay ahead. Ryan imagined jumping into the fresh water and splashing it on his face while slurping water from his cupped hands. He then thought about the fresh berries next to the stream that he would pick and savor with every bite.

Matthew couldn't keep his mind from wandering into a new peaceful vision of having a full stomach and lying down in a bed of fresh leaves. He had tried so hard to stay focused, but as they got closer, he could almost taste the water and fresh berries and feel the coolness of the stream washing over his exhausted body.

Eventually, the sound of running water became even more real with each step. As the sound of the trickling water grew stronger, the energy the boys felt intensified. When they pulled apart the last curtain of vines, they could not believe what they saw!

CHAPTER

The boys were staring at the most luscious area they had ever seen with their own eyes. It was so beautiful it almost took their breath away! Not only had they found the small stream they heard from the distance for the past several hours, but it was surrounded by a grove of huge jungle trees that seemed to be as big as skyscrapers. Beautiful flowers covered the jungle floor and spread over the edges of the stream.

"Wow! The whole ground looks like a unicorn farted rainbow flowers all over it. This is so amazing, I almost peed my pants!" Ryan said as he stared with wide eyes at the beauty surrounding them.

He never imagined there would be a place like this inside what appeared to be such a dangerous jungle. There were so many different kinds of flowers and so many vibrant colors. It was almost hypnotizing to look at.

"I agree with you on that one, as weird as you made that sound," Matthew exclaimed as he too was mesmerized by the beauty of the vibrant covering of the jungle floor.

Ryan took off running toward the stream, and it was exactly

as he had envisioned this moment while making the long hike through the jungle. He suddenly forgot about the past few days and his energy returned full force. He hurdled the fallen branches and rotted trees and crushed the beautiful flowers as his feet pounded against the jungle floor. The closer he got to the stream, the softer the ground became. He noticed his shoes becoming soggy, but he didn't care. Nothing could stop him, and he continued toward the stream at a more rapid pace.

"Ryan, stop! Don't keep moving. There might be a trap. This is too perfect to be true. Whoever put us here might have wanted to trick us into thinking that we have reached a safe place," Matthew said as he stopped dead in his tracks.

Ryan couldn't have cared less about what Matthew had to say at this point, as he was already in the stream dousing himself with the fresh water. He could hardly breathe between the huge gulps of water he took as he cupped his hands and brought the water up to his mouth.

"Matthew, come join me. The water is fine. In fact, it's better than fine. It's perfect!" Ryan said as he swung his arm through the shallow water, attempting to create a splashing wave toward his friend.

Matthew couldn't resist the urge for fresh water. He gave up his crazy idea that it might be a trap and proceeded to follow his friend into the stream. He jumped in and took his first gulp of the water and felt the refreshing water trickling down and pooling deep within his empty stomach.

"Now we just need some food to go along with this water," Matthew said as he sent a splash back into Ryan's face.

"Hey! I'll get you for that. You just wait and see!" Ryan said as he sent another splash back at Matthew's face.

The boys realized how much fun they were having; they wanted to stay in the stream for a long time and just hang out. It was truly the first time they had lost track of where they were, why they were there, and what awful circumstances they had been encountering over the past few days.

"Hey! I have a great idea. Why don't we try to see if we can catch some fish so we can eat some real food? Then we won't be hungry anymore, and I bet it will taste really good," Ryan said as he jumped up and down in the water, excited about his brilliant idea.

Matthew stopped gulping down the water for a moment and responded with less enthusiasm, "There are three things wrong with that idea. The first thing is that we don't have a fishing rod or hooks or string or bait or even a spear. All we have is the puny little knife. The second is that the stream is too shallow in some spots for any fish to live in it. And, the third thing wrong with that idea is that even if we somehow could catch a fish, we wouldn't have anything to cook it on."

Ryan was taken back by Matthew's sudden negative response to what Ryan felt was a legitimate idea. He was simply trying to be helpful and brainstorm an idea for food. He knew that both of them were exhausted and starving, especially after the intensity of the hike to get as far as they were in the jungle, but he certainly didn't expect Matthew to be so harsh.

"Well! That was a major buzzkill, Mr. Killer of Dreams. I was just trying to brainstorm things that we could eat so we could avoid death by starvation by tomorrow morning. You don't need to be so rude!" Ryan stated with frustration.

Matthew was now confused. Despite everything the boys had gone through, it was not like Ryan to be so overcome with emotion, and it was certainly not like him to lose his cool over something as simple as this. Matthew wondered what had gotten into Ryan. It couldn't simply be exhaustion and hunger because they had felt that way for so long already. Whatever it was, Matthew felt he needed to just let it settle as it was and not stir the pot anymore.

"Jeez, dude! No need to get worked up about it. I was just saying that it wouldn't work out, that's all. I wasn't trying to offend you or burst your fish bubble," Matthew said jokingly as he shot his hands up in the air like he was surrendering.

"Sorry, man. I don't know what came over me. It was like I wasn't in control of my body, I was so mad. It was the weirdest feeling. It almost felt like someone was controlling me. Maybe it's just my hunger and exhaustion that are finally getting the best of me," Ryan said as he held his hands out in front of him and rotated them up and down to make sure he could still control himself and hadn't somehow turned into a robot.

Stranger things had been happening, Ryan thought to himself, *so he wouldn't be surprised if whoever put him and Matthew on this island had the power to control their thoughts and actions.* The thought of it sent chills up and down his spine; after reflecting on that thought for a moment, he shook it off and brought himself back to the stream and the conversation with Matthew. It was clear that both of them just needed to chill and move on.

"I think we should head upstream to see what's at the source of the stream. Hopefully, it's a lake so we can have a huge supply of water and a place to camp out for the night. Maybe we can even find some fish or other food," Matthew said, trying to convince Ryan of his plan.

"I think that's a good idea. We should probably head out before it gets dark and we can't see anymore. If we are lucky, we might not need to camp on the shore. Maybe there will be a cave or some kind of shelter where we can sleep," Ryan said, suddenly excited about leaving the beautiful field of flowers and the fresh stream.

The boys started moving along the stream heading toward its source and were hopeful about finding a place of shelter for the night. In the distance, they thought they could see a clearing, but they quickly realized the stream was flowing downhill from a steep incline and it would take them a while to reach the peak of the hill. Both boys were refreshed from the spring water they were able to drink and douse themselves with, but as they made their way up the steep hill, their empty stomachs began to call out to them. As if they needed a reminder that it had been hours again since they had last eaten. They could literally hear each other's stomachs growling and they knew they would have to stop soon to eat their last packet of food if they wanted to have enough energy to make it up the hill.

Out of breath and with fatigue quickly setting in, they both stopped without even having to speak a word. They found a fallen tree to sit on and took off their backpacks to search for another food packet. Although they were so tired of the food packets, they knew this would be their last meal until they found another source of food. Despite the awful taste, they ripped their packets open and started eating them like a Thanksgiving feast.

"Dang it! We should have taken a break so we could have

conserved more energy instead of having to dig into our last food packet this soon," Matthew said with frustration as he kicked his backpack around. "At least we are getting closer to the top of the hill. There has to be food at the top of the hill or we are dead for sure."

"Dude, stop! Just calm down and breathe. Don't have a spaz attack! We will make it up the hill and there will be food at the top. Just trust it will be there when we need it," Ryan said as he gently punched Matthew on his shoulder and kept eating his food packet.

Ryan was enjoying the feeling of the food in his stomach and was grateful for both the food and the opportunity to rest after hiking up the steep hill. Although he was nervous about having to find another food source, the feeling of food landing in the pit of his stomach was something he hadn't felt for a long time now, and he was simply savoring the moment.

"You're right. Let's just keep going and get up to the top of this hill so we can get our food. Then maybe I can cheer up a bit," Matthew said as he got up and brushed the dirt and dried tree bark off his worn pants.

They zipped up their backpacks, slipped their arms through the straps to place them on their backs, and once again began the long trudge up the hill with the hope and prayer of a beautiful lake, fresh fish, orchards of fresh fruit trees, and a large cave for shelter for the night. All there, free for the taking. Matthew imagined both of them rolling around in a field of flowers, similar to the field they found at the bottom of the hill, celebrating their victory of the climb and their discovery of a bountiful harvest. This just had to be everything they had hoped for…

CHAPTER

As the boys got closer to the top of the hill, they picked up the pace, eager to unveil their vision. However, as they reached the top, they were shocked! The reality of what they discovered quickly set in like a sharp knife stabbing them in the gut. It was nothing like they had imagined. Instead of there being a lake, there was a muddy swamp with flies buzzing around. Instead of fruit trees, there were rotted old swamp trees with no fruit on them. How could this be possible? Where did the fresh water come from in the stream they were dousing themselves in downhill if this was the source?

"Seriously? We hiked up that huge hill just to get up to a swamp. I'm so mad! Look at my hands. They are shaking out of control," Ryan said as he threw his backpack on the ground and sat on the trunk of a fallen tree.

Ryan sat with his head in his hands and kicked the ground. He wanted this terrible nightmare to go away. He wanted to go back to wherever it was that he came from; he knew it had to be a million times better than where they were currently at. He lifted his head from his hands and started to look up to the sky to call out to God to save him and his best friend from this terrible place. Suddenly, out of the corner of his eye, he saw something interesting.

"Hey! What is that? Matthew, can you see it? It is right behind that huge tree on the other side of the swamp," Ryan said, pointing excitedly in the direction of the mysterious object he saw.

Matthew examined the object across the swamp and said, "It looks like a giant stone pillar coming out of the ground. Let's go and see what's over there."

"Good idea. Maybe there is something over there that can help us get out of this jungle and off this island," Ryan said as he stood up and put his backpack on.

Ryan finished looking up at the sky to thank God for hearing his cry, even though he had never finished his plea. He was suddenly hopeful that the exploration of this stone pillar would get them one step closer to getting off the island. The boys took off, practically sprinting, to make their way around the swamp toward the pillar. Suddenly, both boys face planted into something in front of them. It was like they had hit a brick wall, and both of them were knocked down flat onto their butts. They were both startled and looked at each other with confusion as they carefully stood back up and looked ahead but saw nothing in front of them.

They started walking again, this time more cautiously since they didn't know what they had hit. Had they really hit something? Could there be a glass wall? But why would there be a glass wall in the middle of the jungle? There had to be something there. But where? They couldn't see anything other than the stone pillar they were headed toward.

Determinedly trying again, they made their way toward the stone pillar. Both boys repeated the face plant into the invisible wall and fell over once again. They shook their heads and looked at each other, this time a bit more confused and even more frightened.

"What the heck! It's like there's an invisible wall in front of us, and every time we try to walk toward that stone pillar, it appears," Matthew said with confusion, and then proceeded to exclaim, "Hey! I have an idea. How about we throw a rock and see where the invisible wall is. If the rock is deflected, then we know for sure where the wall is instead of having to use our faces for the experiment."

Matthew didn't know what to do beyond identifying the location of the wall, but he knew they couldn't just stand there and keep smashing their faces into the invisible wall. He picked up a rock and threw it at the place where he thought the invisible wall was. As he did, the rock simply traveled freely through the air and landed in some brush in the distance. He looked at Ryan with confusion since he thought for sure this would have worked.

Without saying a word, Ryan picked up a rock and attempted the same process. This time, he threw the rock even harder and then ducked, expecting the rock to deflect back at him. Instead, the rock traveled further than the one Matthew had thrown and landed in the distant brush.

The boys stuck their hands out in front of them like mimes trying to find the wall, or whatever it was, that was now holding them hostage and barricading them from reaching the stone pillar. When they reached out, they simply felt air. Attempting another step forward, however, proved the same fate as they were abruptly stopped by the invisible force.

Matthew looked at Ryan and started to recall the events of the past few days in which every time they were faced with a challenge or an obstacle they had to overcome, when they tried to do it on their own, they were stuck. But, when they worked together, they had conquered the obstacle. It was all starting to make sense now. With excitement, Matthew reached down and grabbed two rocks and handed one to his best friend.

"On the count of three, we are both going to throw our rocks at the invisible wall," Matthew declared excitedly to Ryan.

Ryan took the rock with less enthusiasm, but followed the direction of his friend. Both looked at each other and then at the area where they believed the wall to be. They cocked their arms back like major league baseball players on the pitching mound gearing up for a full count, bottom of the ninth, bases loaded situation. On the count of three, they chucked the rocks simultaneously as hard as they could and then ducked.

As they ducked, they carefully turned their heads in the direction they had thrown the rocks and peeked their eyes out from behind their arms that were shielding them from the rocks they expected to deflect back at them. Instead, they could not believe what they were seeing. The invisible wall suddenly opened up and revealed a whole new world in front of them!

They saw an old temple with two gold statues in front, glimmering in the late afternoon sun. The boys could not tell what the statues looked like because of the distance between them and the statues. For the moment they didn't care, though, because they were distracted by the food packets and bottles of water they saw in the center of a circular group of stone pillars off to the side of the golden statues.

The sunlight was illuminating the food packets and water, and it was as if they had been placed there by heavenly angels. The boys were once again drooling at the prospect of something to eat. The way the sunlight danced off the packets and reflected beams of light through the bottles, they just couldn't resist any longer. At this point, the food and water were far more precious than the mysterious golden statues, as they realized that gold would certainly not do them any good if they died of starvation.

Ryan was the first to act and started running toward the temple at full speed while he was pointing and shouting, "Look at that group of stone pillars over there. It looks like there are food packets and water in the middle of it. Let's go get it!"

"Wait! It might be a trap. Stop right now!" Matthew said as he took off running so he could chase down Ryan, hoping to stop him from encountering any potential traps. "Oh, come on! I always have to chase you down, Ryan. Why can't you just listen for once? Ugh!" he exclaimed with intensity as he continued to chase after Ryan.

"Everything to you is a trap," shouted Ryan as he huffed and puffed out of breath, but continued to forge ahead toward the food and water.

Ryan had not hesitated, despite Matthew's attempt at another warning. He ran right past the golden statues and headed straight toward the circular group of stone pillars where the food packets and water were just waiting for him. When Ryan finally reached them, he picked them up and began kissing them.

Ryan turned to look for Matthew, and as he did, he felt the

ground begin to shake. The smile that had been plastered on Ryan's face turned quickly into an expression of fear. He hugged them tightly and suddenly there was a loud bang! The ground began to fall away from the center of the stone pillars and he watched with fear as the stone pillars fell into the deep chasm of nothingness. All that remained was a small circular platform where Ryan was standing, desperately clutching the food packets and water.

"Matthew! What's happening? What happened to the ground?" Ryan shouted as he trembled with fear.

As he was calling out to Matthew, he continued to scan his surroundings. It was then that he realized Matthew had stopped right at the edge of where the ground had fallen away. If Matthew hadn't hesitated and stopped to warn Ryan, he would have been a goner, falling deep into the gaping hole in front of him.

Ryan was truly scared since he could feel the platform shifting gently below his feet. He didn't know how much longer he had before the platform crumbled and fell into the same deep hole, but he knew that if he wanted to make it back to solid ground and to Matthew, he would have to jump.

"Are you okay, Ryan? Did you get hurt?" Matthew shouted with concern in his voice as he looked down into the large gaping hole right in front of his feet.

"Yes! I'm fine; I'm not hurt. But I am going to have to jump off this platform to get back on that side of the hole," Ryan said.

Ryan continued to focus on keeping his balance as he surveyed where Matthew was standing and tried to measure the distance between them. It had to be at least a six-foot gap in between the platform he was on and the other side of the hole, the solid ground where Matthew was standing. Ryan didn't know if he could jump and make it to the other side. Fear and doubt overtook his mind, and he began to imagine himself falling deep into the hole.

"Come on! You are going to have to jump, Ryan, and you need to do it quickly before that platform gives out. You can make it, Ryan!" Matthew shouted across the hole and then added, "I'm pretty sure a three-year-old could jump further than that!"

Matthew hoped the little dig he provided to his best friend would be what it would take to get Ryan angry enough to jump further than the distance he needed to make it across the gaping hole. Despite the fact that Matthew was on solid ground, he had an intense fear of Ryan not being able to make it across, leaving him alone on the island. He couldn't bear the thought of losing his best friend.

Matthew cupped his hands over his mouth and shouted two more commands to Ryan, "Carefully put the food packets and water into your backpack, and then before you jump, imagine yourself as an Olympic long jumper flying through the air. You can do it!"

Ryan knew that Matthew was right. He remembered hearing about athletes who visualized over and over winning a competition or making a successful shot; he knew he had to shift from thoughts of failure and focus on the success he was about to have. He imagined himself sailing through the air and landing safely on the other side.

As he focused on these new, positive thoughts, he carefully

took his backpack off, unzipped it slowly, and gently placed the food packets and water inside. He was worried about the extra weight on his back, but he knew this might be their only chance of having anything to eat again for a while. He knew that if he didn't take the food, they would die of starvation. It was a risk he had to take.

"Okay! I'm going to jump across!" Ryan shouted as he took a couple of steps back. He was now as close to the edge of the platform as he could get, so his running start would be limited to only a few steps. He took a deep breath and started running forward. He took a running leap…For a second, he thought he was going to make it, but then quickly realized he was going to fall short.

He reached his hands up and, at the last second, grabbed the edge of the hole. His legs were dangling freely into the deep hole, and he could feel the weight of his backpack tugging him down. He was clinging desperately, trying to dig his fingers into the dirt at the top of the deep hole and was barely hanging on. Suddenly, the dirt on the ledge began to give way and his fingers started to slip!

CHAPTER  8

Just as Ryan's fingers slipped off the dirt ledge, Matthew dove onto his belly at the edge of the hole and grabbed onto Ryan's hands! Matthew thought his weight would be enough to hold both of them, but his body started creeping toward Ryan and the edge of the hole, and he just couldn't stop it. He was slowly sliding closer to the edge of the hole, and the grip he had on Ryan's hands was beginning to give way.

Suddenly, Matthew felt his right foot hook onto something solid and his body stopped sliding. He regained his grip on Ryan's hands and pulled desperately. He barely had enough strength to pull Ryan up onto the edge of the cliff, but with every last ounce of effort, he tugged as hard as he could, and it was enough to bring Ryan close enough to be able to lift his right leg onto the solid ground.

Matthew pulled and Ryan pushed his body up onto the ledge. Both boys collapsed backward onto the solid ground with exhaustion. Ryan rolled onto his stomach to avoid crushing his backpack, and the boys lay there silent for what felt like an eternity, their chests heaving up and down with their bodies pressed firmly against the earth. Never had the ground felt so good. Neither of them had enough energy to speak.

"Well, I'm sure glad you caught me, dude," Ryan said finally, as he broke the silence.

The boys looked at each other and started laughing harder than they ever had since they had been on the island. It felt as though they were going to bust a lung. Laughing and lying on the ground was the therapy both needed, as the stress of the last few moments was more than they thought they could handle.

Matthew rolled onto his side, pushed himself up, and said, "Wow! Next time, let's talk before you go running off. If it wasn't for my foot catching that tree root over there, we would both be goners."

Ryan sat up and responded, "Okay, I'm pretty sure I have offcially learned my lesson this time."

Ryan took his backpack off his back and started to unzip it. As he did, his hands continued to shake, and he could feel the adrenaline rush still pulsating through his body. He definitely didn't expect to have been in that spot. He was so thankful for Matthew saving his butt once again. He started to tally up the saves in his mind and then decided that since he had been given another chance, he would start to work more closely with Matthew and make decisions together before running off.

Ryan reached down into the backpack and pulled out the packets of food and water. He felt relieved that he had listen to Matthew and decided to pack them while suspended on that platform. It was another reminder to him that he always needed to think ahead and listen to his gut instinct.

"Well, we better not let this food go to waste. Let's eat," Ryan said as he displayed the food packets and water as if they were as precious as gold.

"Ooh! Yummy! Chopped liver paste. My favorite," Matthew said sarcastically as he grabbed the packet and took a huge bite. "This was totally worth you almost dying for!"

"Ha! Ha! Very funny, but no, it wasn't," Ryan said as he frowned at Matthew in between bites of food.

Ryan was truly grateful for Matthew saving his life, but now he wasn't going to admit it to him otherwise he would get a big head.

"I know. I was just kidding and trying to lighten up the mood," Matthew said as he took another bite of his food. Matthew could feel the strength returning to his body with every bite, despite the awful taste, and he noticed that his body was no longer shaking as it had been after he pulled Ryan to safety. As the boys sat there eating their food and drinking their water, Matthew began to look around, and the glimmer of the gold statues they had originally seen caught his eye again.

"Hey! Those two gold statues are still over there," Matthew said as he pointed in the direction of the shining objects.

Although the stone pillars had fallen into the deep hole and were no longer near the old temple, the gold statues remained standing in the middle of a grove of jungle trees surrounded by hanging vines and moss next to the temple. The boys were closer to the statues now, but they could still not see the details of the carving. With the way the ground had been shaking, they couldn't believe the statues were still standing.

"Let's go over and check it out. Maybe there will be more food," Ryan said as he started to pack up his belongings.

"Don't you dare. Do not go running off again," Matthew responded sternly as he stared at Ryan, remembering what had just happened when Ryan ran off without him.

"I know! I know! I won't run off again. I learned my lesson last time I did that. I almost died," Ryan said as he looked back toward the pit where he almost fell to his death.

The boys packed up their backpacks, stood up, brushed themselves off once again, and started walking toward the shining objects in the ground in front of them. As they made their way in the direction of the gold statues, they were careful to keep a solid distance between themselves and the gaping hole in the ground that had just been created after capturing the food packets and water.

As they got closer to the objects, they saw several small pieces of gold sticking out of the ground. Matthew reached down and picked up a piece of gold and examined it, wondering if it was truly the real thing. If so, what was it doing here? Someone had to have been here before them. But who? Who was behind all of this?

With so many questions dancing in their heads, the boys continued to make their way through the jungle toward the golden statues. As they got closer, they began to appreciate how big the statues were. They were life size, just slightly bigger than each of the boys, and they appeared to have faces carved into them.

As they walked around to the front of the statues, the boys gasped in shock at what they saw. The faces on the golden statues looked just like Matthew and Ryan. In fact, they were perfect replicas.

"What the heck! Why do these statues look like us? This is creeping me out," Ryan said as he walked up to the statue that resembled him and touched it on its arm.

The golden statue felt really warm, almost like someone had just melted it into its shape. Ryan pulled his hand back quickly as it felt so strange to be touching something that looked like him, was warm like a real human, and yet was made of gold. Nothing made sense about this. In fact, nothing made sense about this entire journey they were on.

"I don't know why the statues look like us," Matthew said as he reached out to touch his statue.

It too felt like someone had recently melted it into shape. As he pressed harder, his hand melted into it like he was touching warm butter. He gasped as he saw his hand disappear into the statue, and he quickly pulled it back.

"This is crazy! It feels like butter when you press your hand into it, and my hand completely disappeared when I pressed into it," Matthew said nervously as he began to examine his hand.

Matthew discovered there was no residue on his hand when he pulled it out of the statue, but he was still in shock over what had just happened. Maybe this was just a hallucination. He looked over to where Ryan was standing just as Ryan began to press his hand against the hand of his golden twin statue. Matthew saw Ryan's arm disappear; suddenly, Ryan had disappeared into the statue too!

"Ryan! Can you hear me?" Matthew screamed into the face of Ryan's golden statue as he looked around in a panic.

By the time he had gotten over to Ryan's twin statue, it was too late. He was gone. Ryan had disappeared into his golden twin statue, and Matthew realized Ryan wasn't coming back. How could this be happening? Matthew was so confused. He didn't know what to do.

He pressed against Ryan's statue, but it was cold and hard as a rock. It was not like when he had touched his own golden twin. He needed to somehow get to Ryan, but realized Ryan's statue would not allow him passage into whatever world Ryan had been sucked into.

Matthew ran back over to his own golden twin and gently touched his hand on the hand of the statue. This time, instead of resisting and pulling back, he closed his eyes and pushed his body forward into the body of his statue. He could feel himself being sucked in and suddenly the pitch black turned into a bright light as he emerged on the other side.

He squinted and cautiously opened one eye at a time and dropped his arms down as they had been serving as his only protection as he had crossed into the other world. It was then that he saw Ryan standing there staring at a huge temple covered in moss.

Ryan turned around, grinned at Matthew, and calmly said, "Hey, dude, what took you so long? I've been waiting forever."

Matthew thought Ryan was unusually calm considering the fact he had just gotten sucked into a new world through a golden twin statue. He apparently had no idea that Matthew thought he was dying inside the statue.

"What took me so long? I thought you were dying inside your statue. I tried to come rescue you. When I tried to get through your twin statue, it was cold and hard as a rock, kinda like your brain!" Matthew yelled as he pointed back toward the area he had magically entered this strange world, and then went on to say, "Again, you should have told me you were going to step inside the statue. Then maybe I wouldn't be freaking out right now."

"Sorry, dude! I didn't mean to freak you out. I just wanted to see what the statue felt like. The next thing I knew, I was on the other side, and I couldn't get back to you. On the plus side, I found this awesome temple," Ryan said as he pointed toward the temple.

Matthew had been so distracted by the transport, and then the anger that overcame him from Ryan running off again on his own, that he completely disregarded the amazing temple that was right in front of them. He was apparently too busy yelling at Ryan to even appreciate the discovery.

Matthew and Ryan stood facing the temple and realized it was quite a bit larger than the one they had seen on the "other side." It had a similar design, but this one was more intricate with stone pillars supporting a grand entry. Moss and branches were hanging from the top of the roof. There were seven steps that led up to the door of the temple and it had to be at least three stories high. In the distance, the boys saw the same huge volcano they had seen from the beach, so they knew they were still on the island; they just weren't sure where on the island the statues had taken them.

Matthew stopped gazing at the temple and looked at Ryan and said, "It's okay. I was just afraid that I would be alone on the island. That's something I really don't want to happen to either of us." He looked back at the temple and continued, "Anyway, that temple looks pretty cool. Do you know what's in it?"

Matthew asked as he looked back at Ryan.

"Nope. I didn't dare go take a sneak peek without my best buddy, but I think we should go and find out. This time, we should walk side by side instead of me running off and getting us into more trouble," Ryan said while he had a quick flashback from the past few events.

"Good idea! If we stick together nothing should go wrong. Right?" Matthew responded as he and Ryan stood there staring at their next adventure.

CHAPTER

They started walking cautiously toward the temple's grand entrance. With each step they climbed, they could feel their own heart rate accelerating; they thought for sure they could hear each other's heart beating outside of their chests. They reached the top of the stone steps and gazed up at the massive stone door in front of them.

Moss was hanging down all around them and they brushed it away with a sweeping motion like they had used when they entered the jungle through the thick curtain of leaves and branches. They continued to move toward the door, careful not to disturb anything around them. Without speaking, both reached out to grab the old handle on the stone door and pulled at the same time to open the heavy door to the temple.

As they stepped inside, they saw a huge chest in the middle of the floor, and vines hanging from the ceiling. There were stone seats positioned in a circular fashion all around the perimeter of the temple; it looked similar to an old cathedral or church. One that had been overtaken by what looked like a spider web of thick vines.

"Cool!" Ryan whispered as he and Matthew started walking toward the chest in the middle of the floor.

Matthew took the first step and as he did, they heard a loud click! The floor started moving apart, revealing a pit full of lava under them. The boys looked at each other and at their surroundings, frantically looking for a way to escape.

"Ah! Look, the floor is spreading apart!" Ryan yelled as he jumped onto one side of the floor as it separated beneath his feet.

Not again, he thought to himself as he saw Matthew jump onto the other side of the divided floor. The ground continued to tremble until the floor had completely divided. Another loud bang signaled the end of the division, and there was no longer a floor beneath them! Ryan looked around him at all the vines hanging from the ceiling and now suspended across the lava pit and realized their lives were now suspended only by the strength of the vines. If the vines gave way, they would fall to their death in the lava pit.

The boys were now both standing on the suspended vines above the lava pit and were hanging on to the vines that were coming down from the ceiling of the temple. The floor was no longer beneath them, and the only way for them to get out of the temple was to cross the vines to make their way out of the temple.

"We are going to have to jump from vine to vine to stay above the lava," Ryan hollered across the room to Matthew, who apparently had already had the same idea as he was already hanging desperately onto a vine.

Matthew shouted and nodded his head in the direction of the back of the temple, "We are too far away from the entrance where we came in, but I think I see another door toward the back."

Ryan looked in the direction Matthew was motioning to with his head and saw what he also thought might be another way out of the temple. They each started sliding their feet carefully across the vines while hanging on to the vines that were suspended from the ceiling. It was as if they were tightrope walkers in a circus, except there was no net below to catch them if they fell. This was life or death.

As they continued to make their way closer to the back of the temple, Matthew realized they had forgotten about the chest they had seen in the center of the room. The chest was what they were originally going after when they entered the temple. They couldn't leave it behind. He looked to his right and saw the chest suspended in a network of vines in the center of the temple in the same location it had originally been.

Matthew stopped moving toward the back and instead turned his body to the right and began moving in the direction of the chest. This time it was he who had strayed from Ryan, but he felt as if he was being pulled to the chest.

"I'll go for the chest and see what's inside. You head to the back and see if you can find a way out of this temple. Wait for me there," Matthew said as he kept his eyes glued to the network of vines he was maneuvering on to get to the chest. After what seemed like hours, he finally reached the chest. As he balanced his feet between two vines and hung onto one vine with his left hand, he carefully let go of the vine he was hanging onto with his right hand. He gently leaned forward and bent down to reach the top of the chest. He unlatched the top and lifted it open. Matthew was shocked by what he saw.

It was a small wooden key lying in the very center of the chest.

He reached down, picked it up, and shoved it into his pocket. He then carefully closed the lid after looking again to see if there was anything else inside. He had hoped there would be food or water or something they could actually find to be useful at this point.

But instead, there was only a key. *What would they do with a key?* he thought to himself as he began to make his way toward the back of the temple. He could see Ryan standing and waving his arms at him, motioning for Matthew to come back toward him. Matthew had a lot of time to think while he traversed the vines, but he reminded himself that he should not dwell on the stupid key, but rather stay focused on not falling off the vines. He could see the lava beneath him and feel the heat coming from the pit below. It was more than enough to keep him focused.

Ryan was standing at the back of the temple on a platform near a door. He couldn't wait to get the heck out of this strange temple. Even though he was now on the solid ground, he still did not feel safe. He had seen Matthew open the chest but couldn't see what was in it. He hoped it was something useful like food or water.

As Matthew got closer, Ryan began motioning to him to hurry. Matthew looked exhausted and Ryan knew the heat from the lava pit and the extra effort he had made to get to the chest were the causes of the exhaustion. Once Matthew got close enough to the platform, he dove off the vines and landed next to Ryan at the back of the temple. He made it.

"Dude, that was so hard. I'm exhausted," Matthew said out of breath as he flopped down onto the platform and started breathing heavily while lying there on the ground.

Matthew's body was telling him to stay on the platform, as it felt cool and comforting, but his mind was telling him they needed to get out of the temple quickly. Who knew what was going to happen next if they stayed inside the temple? It was definitely time to move.

"Let's keep moving," Matthew said as he stood up and started walking toward the door Ryan had found at the back of the temple.

As they exited the temple, Matthew handed Ryan his backpack then tried to sit down on a log that was just outside the temple door. Ryan had not seen Matthew this exhausted before, but he knew they needed to keep moving.

"Come on. We have to keep moving until we find a safe place to sleep," Ryan said as he pulled Matthew to his feet.

Ryan pressed on to keep walking forward and Matthew stumbled along behind him. Ryan was hoping to find a cave or a grove of trees to sleep in, as the sun was starting to set in front of them. It felt like one of the longest days they had since they arrived on the island, and they could definitely feel the exhaustion enveloping their entire bodies.

The boys finally reached a grove of trees with a small stream flowing alongside. The sound of the trickling water was inviting. For the first time since they had reached the original stream, they started to feel a sense of calm come over them. They explored the area to ensure it was safe and could provide enough shelter, and they decided to settle in as best they could for the night.

Although the area didn't provide them as much protection as they had hoped, they knew they absolutely needed some rest and their bodies could not tolerate any more. Neither of them had any idea what would lie ahead if they decided to press on. This was definitely their best bet for some sleep for the night.

Ryan grabbed both of the backpacks and began to dig out the supplies, including the blankets and the last packets of food and bottles of water. Ryan was again so thankful he had gone after the food packets and water at the small temple. He actually had a sense of pride come over him as he realized he had risked his life to save his best friend and himself from starvation. Although the moment of pride felt amazing, Ryan could feel the fatigue continue to overtake his body.

As Ryan continued to unpack the supplies, he looked over at Matthew, who was sitting on the ground under a tree. Just as Ryan looked over at him, Matthew started to look really pale and suddenly collapsed on the ground next to Ryan's feet. "Matthew, are you okay? Dude, answer me!" Ryan yelled.

Ryan grabbed Matthew's shoulders and shook him, but it was not working. Matthew was not waking up. Ryan reached into his backpack and pulled out his cup. He dipped it into the trickling stream and filled it with water. He then quickly splashed the cold water onto Matthew's pale face and Matthew sprang to life.

Matthew sat up, startled, and tried to wipe the water from his face and exclaimed, "What happened? All I remember was falling, then everything went black."

"You passed out on me," Ryan said as he was dipping the cup in the stream for another round of splashing if required.

Matthew put his arms up to protect himself from Ryan's next water toss and said, "Put the water down, Ryan. I'm fine now. I think I just need some food and water and I will feel better. And then, we need to get some sleep."

"Exactly my thoughts, and that's what I was working on until you took a nosedive on me, buddy," Ryan said as he picked up one of the food packets and chucked it in the direction of Matthew.

The boys opened their food packets and bottles of water and savored another meal. This was again the last of the food packets, and based on the way their journey had gone so far, they expected that if they were to be able to eat again, they would likely have to conquer yet another obstacle. Neither wanted to even think about what might be in store for them as they had still not gotten comfortable with the uncertainty of this adventure. The real question was, would they ever be comfortable with uncertainty?

As Matthew was pondering the next step of their journey, he remembered something. He remembered he had discovered the mysterious key inside the chest in the temple. In fact, he had risked his life to get that key, yet he had forgotten to tell Ryan about it. Matthew reached into his pocket and pulled out the wooden key. He breathed a sigh of relief as he had completely forgotten about it. For all he knew, he could have dropped it along the way as they were scrambling to get out of the temple.

"Hey, I forgot to show you what I found inside the chest in the temple," Matthew said as he held up the old wooden key.

Ryan crawled over to where Matthew was sitting and took the key from Matthew. He examined every angle of the key, turning it upside down and around from front to back. They could both see it had small wooden carvings marked into it, but they could not make out what the carvings said. It must have been in some other language, or maybe it had just worn off as the key looked like it was centuries old.

"What do you think this key is for?" Matthew said as he took the key back from Ryan.

"I'm not sure. Maybe it was to unlock some secret room in the temple, but all I found when I looked around, even before the floor split, was the back door where we left," Ryan continued, "or maybe it has something to do with that small wooden box that was on the boat. Maybe the key would have opened up the box, but now we will never know since my shark friend has likely enjoyed it as a snack," Ryan said as he flashed a quick grin at his friend.

"Well, whatever it is, and whatever it is for, I think we should hold onto it and keep it safe and maybe tomorrow we will find some purpose for it," Matthew said as he laid his head down onto his backpack.

"Yep. Right on," Ryan said as he settled in and grabbed his blanket.

Tonight there would be no fire to keep them warm. It was just Ryan and Matthew under the grove of trees in the jungle.

...Or was it?

CHAPTER

Cock-a-doodle-doo! Reggie crowed for the traditional morning alarm. Both boys were so familiar with the sound, they did not startle this time. Instead, Matthew rolled over onto his back with his eyes still closed. Something definitely seemed different, though, this morning.

As Matthew rolled over, he could hear the heaving sound of deep breaths and feel the warmth of the breath on his face. There was a terrible smell. He thought it was Ryan sharing his awful morning breath with him. It had been days of food packets and no toothbrush; the thought of it and the nasty smell of the hot breath made Matthew want to gag. This was not the way he wanted to wake up this morning after all they had already gone through.

With his eyes still closed and pretending to be sleeping, Matthew reached up to slap what he thought was Ryan's face. What he felt though was nothing like Ryan's face. It felt like matted, tough fur.

Matthew quickly opened his eyes and realized it wasn't Ryan breathing on him. Through the bright sunlight shining down, he could see the sun illuminating something that was much scarier and much uglier than Ryan. It was some sort of animal!

Just then, Matthew heard Ryan scream, "Ah! Dude! There's a beast breathing on your face!"

The beast was the ugliest creature Ryan had ever seen. It looked like a cross between a lion and a bull, with the head of a lion and horns and body of a bull. It had dark matted fur, and Ryan noticed that its feet had razor sharp claws like a lion. He knew this "thing" was not going to play nice, and the last thing he wanted to do was go anywhere near it. However, he also knew that Matthew desperately needed his help and a distraction to lure the beast away before Matthew became its breakfast.

Ryan quickly jumped up, reached into his backpack, and threw his cup at the beast, hoping to lure it away from Matthew, who was in a helpless position with the beast hovering over him. As Ryan chucked the cup at the beast and started running to find a place to hide, the beast turned his head sharply and took off in Ryan's direction.

For a split second when the beast took off toward Ryan, Matthew was blinded by the sunlight that hit his face. He sat up and grabbed his backpack, hunting for his knife. With trembling hands, he located the knife and pulled it out of his backpack. He quickly got to his feet and waved the knife in the air in an attempt to show Ryan he had some means to fight the beast.

Matthew knew the beast was big, but once he was on his feet, he recognized that the beast was beyond huge! He needed much more than his puny knife to fight this thing off. He needed a strategy, and he needed to figure it out quickly because the beast was charging directly toward Ryan. Without hesitating,

Matthew ran after the beast, desperately trying to save his best friend once again. Matthew jumped up and down and yelled at the top of his lungs to try to distract the beast, just like Ryan had done for him.

"Hey, Ryan! Climb that tree. The beast can't reach you there!" Matthew yelled as he pointed to a tree that was right in front of Ryan.

Matthew also scrambled up a nearby tree. He reached a limb of the tree just out of the beast's reach and saw Ryan was trying to do the same, but the beast was too close. Matthew reached to his side and grabbed onto a smaller branch. He broke it off and threw it at the beast. The beast turned its head and started charging toward Matthew's tree. Matthew hung on to the tree limb tightly with his left arm, dropped down as far as he safely could, and as the beast lunged toward his tree, he reached down with his right arm and stabbed the beast in the neck with his knife. The beast roared in anger and reared up on its hind legs. The beast repeated its charge toward Matthew with an angry snarl and drool streaming across its horrid face.

As the beast drew near Matthew's tree for the second round of attacks, it bucked its head and head-butted the tree so hard Matthew rolled off the limb he had been clinging to. Matthew screamed and started running desperately toward Ryan, flailing his arms and still waving the knife in the air.

"Ryan, help me! I think I made it angry!" Matthew yelled as he finally reached Ryan.

Ryan grabbed Matthew's shoulders and pulled him around behind a tree where he had been hiding. The tree was wide enough to protect both of them for the moment, but not for long. They pressed their backs against the bark of the solid tree and then folded their bodies in half, dropping their hands down to their knees while they gasped for air. Both were trembling and out of breath.

Matthew was still squeezing the knife tightly in his right hand, and he could see what he thought must be the beast's blood, but it was green goo. Matthew could not believe what he was seeing. There was no time to ask questions now though. They needed to develop a strategy to get themselves out of yet another mess. They had to conquer this obstacle, and this one would require more than just strength. It would require a true warrior.

For a split second, Matthew had a flashback of his mom and dad talking to him about what it meant to be a warrior. He couldn't quite recall what had happened, but he knew it was bad. They had needed to pull together as a family to overcome a major challenge. He remembered his mom and dad saying things like, "A warrior acts in spite of fear and is willing to do whatever it takes, even if it's hard. A warrior is bigger than any obstacle and never gives up." It was then that Matthew realized that he had to become that warrior, to use intelligence, courage, and strength to overcome this challenge he and Ryan faced.

As Matthew recalled the many obstacles they had already overcome, his adrenaline started to bubble up inside of him, and he could feel himself stepping past the fear and into his own warrior state. He quickly stood up and turned to face Ryan. He grabbed Ryan by the shoulders and pulled him upright to a standing position.

"Ryan, this thing is not real. It's just another challenge; we need to do this together. I will explain later, but you need to climb this tree and distract the beast. Get it to rear up like it did when I made it angry. I will come out from around the tree and stab it in the heart," Matthew said as he knelt down motioning for Ryan to place his foot on Matthew's interlocked hands for a boost up to the first branch of the tree.

Without hesitation, Ryan placed his left foot into Matthew's interlocked hands. With a boost from Matthew, he swung his right leg around the branch and secured himself onto the thick branch. Ryan crawled out a bit further onto the branch as if he was a worm dangling on a fishing line, just waiting to be swallowed whole by a fish. This was unfortunately not an ordinary fish, however. It was Jaws!

Ryan secured himself as far out as he could on the branch and motioned to Matthew that he was ready. Matthew gave the thumbs up and then disappeared behind the tree, opposite the branch where Ryan was dangling for the beast's breakfast.

Ryan broke off a small branch and chucked it in the direction of the beast and hollered, "Ding! Ding! Ding! Come and get it, you big, ugly thing!"

Before Ryan could finish his taunting, the beast came charging toward the tree. Ryan could see it coming and he held on for his life as the beast reared up in an attempt to reach the branch with its head to knock Ryan off.

Ryan squeezed his eyes tightly and screamed, "NOW, Matthew!"

Matthew jumped out from behind the tree, reached up with his knife clenched in his fist, and swung for the chest of the beast. As his arm came down hard, he felt the knife plunge into the beast's chest. He pulled it out of the beast's chest and dove to the ground, crawling back behind the tree just as the beast came down from his hind legs and collapsed onto the ground.

Both of the boys felt the ground shake, and Ryan's branch quivered while he desperately clung to it. Ryan opened his eyes and saw the beast lying on the ground next to the tree. Was it dead? Did their plan work?

Matthew sat with his back against the tree, his head wrapped in his arms and tucked between his knees. He could feel the gooey blood dripping off the knife onto his leg. When he looked up, he saw that it was indeed green. He hadn't been mistaken.

After several minutes of carefully watching the beast, Ryan saw no signs of life coming from it. He started to make his way back down the tree and quietly slid down the tree trunk to the ground next to Matthew. He saw the knife covered in the green goo and knew then what Matthew was talking about when he made the decision to fight the beast. This had to be another challenge that was planned by whoever planted them on the island.

"Oh my gosh. Dude, we killed it. We actually killed it," Ryan said as he picked up a stick and made his way cautiously toward the beast.

Matthew stood up and walked closely next to Ryan. Ryan took the stick and poked the beast in the face from as far away as possible. As he did, the beast's body slowly started to melt away. The boys could not believe what they were seeing! As the beast's body melted, they saw food packets and bottles of water come out of it!

"Now that was disgusting!" Matthew said as he looked at

Ryan, who was staring at the food and water in amazement. He went on to say, "I wonder if the food and water will taste the same knowing it came out of the beast's guts. Do you think for every beast we kill, we will get food and water?"

Matthew was starting to wonder if they should become beast hunters and go kill some more so they could see if each one would give them food and water. He was feeling strong after his quick thinking and after stepping past his fear to conquer the beast. Had he hesitated even for a moment, who knows what the outcome might have been.

"Well, I vote NO for the beast hunting. Yes, there is a possibility they will give us food and water, but there is also a possibility they won't. Besides, I'm not too fond of green goo, and we only have one knife to fight with, so one of us would be defenseless at all times when we are hunting them," Ryan said, promptly pointing out all the flaws in Matthew's idea.

"Yeah. I hear ya. I think we should forgo beast hunting for now. But, if we do face another beast, then we will figure out if my thought was right or not," Matthew said.

For some reason, he was still silently hoping they would stumble upon another beast or maybe even a herd of beasts. What had gotten into him? He actually wanted to fight the beasts? This was all becoming too much to handle. It felt like he was literally becoming a different person. After surviving all these challenges, his confidence was starting to soar, but what he didn't want to do was get too cocky. He knew that could mean bad news for both him and Ryan. As he caught himself thinking these crazy thoughts, he quickly stopped and joined back in the conversation with Ryan.

The boys gathered up the food packets and water and went back to the trees they had slept under, sat down, and had their morning breakfast. This time, they enjoyed the "beast flavored" food packets and grinned from ear to ear as they recalled the frightening morning events. They decided it was definitely not the way they had expected to wake up. Reggie was enough to deal with, but they agreed they would take Reggie as their morning alarm clock over the ugly beast any day.

As they finished up their breakfast, Matthew looked over at Ryan and said, "Your 'girlfriend' sure had bad breath. And, she was uglier than I thought she would be too!"

Ryan stopped chewing for a moment, looked at his best friend, smirked and said, "Really?"

The boys enjoyed a quick laugh over that one and finally finished up their beast breakfast. They had not expected the morning to go that way, but they were thankful they had both survived and were eager to get moving again. They certainly did not want to encounter any more of those "things" along the way.

"Well, let's get a move on. What direction do you think we should go?" Ryan said, and then promptly interrupted again instead of waiting for Matthew's opinion. "I want to go straight ahead because it looks like there's a lot less brush than to the right or the left, and we obviously can't go backward or we will end up back at the temple."

"I really don't think we should go straight because it seems like the obvious path to take. There is no shelter and we would be exposing ourselves to who-knows-what. I think we should either go right or left, and since I'm right-handed, let's go right. It seems like the 'right' thing to do. Get it?" Matthew said laughing at his own humorous response.

Ryan rolled his eyes and said, "Okay. I think you might actually be right about this one. I'm game to head that way." Matthew flashed a quick grin at Ryan and both recognized that whoever was responsible for placing them on the island would probably be trying to mislead them too. It was a risk they would have to take because they knew they needed to keep moving. They not only had to keep finding food and water in this crazy game they were in, but they also needed to find a way off the island.

"Thank you for finally agreeing with me! We should carve it into a tree that you finally listened to me for once," Matthew said as he smiled, picked up his backpack, and they both headed toward the right into the thick jungle brush.

CHAPTER

Matthew was smiling inside because he knew Ryan was actually starting to listen to him. He recognized with each of these challenges they had faced, their friendship continued to grow and they were closer than they had ever been. Each of them had been the support for the other, and they had both been willing to receive help when needed. Matthew didn't know why they were here or what they were supposed to learn from this experience, but he felt like he had already learned so much. He was again so thankful that he was with his best friend.

The boys chopped their way through the jungle brush for what felt like hours. The heat and humidity of the day were starting to intensify, and they could feel the beads of sweat running down their backs behind their backpacks. They knew it wouldn't be long before they would need another break. The food packets were just not enough to sustain their energy for any length of time, but for now, it was all they had.

As they made their way through another thick curtain of jungle vines, they suddenly heard a faint rushing sound. It sounded like rushing water. Like a waterfall! Both boys looked at each other and started moving more quickly toward the sound of rushing water, this time being very careful to stay close to each other in hopes of avoiding any sudden surprises. As they walked along, pushing the jungle brush aside, they started imagining bathing in the cool waterfall and finding some fresh fish and water to fill their empty stomachs. The sound of the water reminded them of the original stream they had found. They remembered how good it felt to splash and drink the cool water.

"Hey, do you hear that? I think there's a waterfall ahead of us. Maybe we can take a shower and get some fresh water and maybe even some fish," Ryan said as he took the knife out of Matthew's hand and started chopping at the vines and brush faster than Matthew had before.

Ryan could not wait to get cleaned up in the water because both he and Matthew were really starting to stink. Especially Matthew. Neither one of them smelled like the fresh flowers they had found when they entered the jungle; Ryan thought Matthew was really starting to smell rotten. He didn't know how much longer he would be able to stand the smell.

As they drew closer to the waterfall, the sound of rushing water continued to intensify. The jungle brush continued to get thicker and thicker, and Ryan had to chop harder than he did before to get through the thick vines, brush, and fallen trees. The prospect of a shower and dunking Matthew's face in the water excited him. It was enough to keep him moving. "Hey, Matthew! Do you want to be a good slave and take a turn chopping vines? My arms are tired," Ryan said to Matthew as he handed the knife back to him.

Matthew started chopping at the brush as hard as he could

while imagining the vines were the beast's face. His imagination continued to wander, and soon he envisioned himself running under the waterfall and dunking Ryan's face into the water. He couldn't wait to get to the waterfall and make that dream come true.

Suddenly, on the next swing, as Matthew chopped into the thick vines, a whole pile of vines, leaves, and moss came tumbling down onto Matthew's head. It got into his clothes, mouth, hair, and completely covered him from head to toe. Ryan was trying so hard not to laugh that his head looked like a bright red balloon filled with air and about to burst.

As Matthew turned around, Ryan couldn't hold it in anymore, "Ha! Ha! You look so funny! It looks like you have moss growing out of your ears and nose. You are uglier than the beast we killed this morning," Ryan exclaimed as he collapsed with laughter and started slapping the ground.

Ryan had tears streaming down his face from laughing so hard. Matthew looked down at Ryan with frustration that his best friend was being a jerk, but then he saw a wet spot start to form across Ryan's pants. Ryan had peed his pants because he was laughing so hard! Matthew recognized this would be the perfect opportunity to get him back.

"I may be ugly, but at least I'm a big boy and don't pee my pants," Matthew said as he picked some of the moss out of his hair and chucked it at Ryan who was still lying on the ground. Ryan stopped the commotion long enough to validate what Matthew was saying. He rolled over and covered himself up. He may have peed his pants, but it was definitely worth it. He hadn't laughed that hard since they had been stranded on the island.

Ryan scowled at Matthew and said, "I'm going to keep moving now so I can get cleaned up in the water. You might want to join me and get cleaned up yourself because you smell like the rotten beast we killed this morning."

Matthew brushed the moss and vines off himself and then helped Ryan back up to his feet. Ryan was right; they were both starting to smell, and he knew the water would feel really good right about now. Matthew and Ryan continued in the direction of the sound of the rushing water. While they made their way through the jungle, Matthew continued to reflect back to the time they arrived on the island and all the challenges they had faced along the way. That brought back some really bad memories, and it seemed like it was already a lifetime ago when they had woken up in this strange place.

"Hey, look! I can see the waterfall!" Matthew pointed ahead as he slashed the last vine, being careful not to get moss all over himself again.

As they cleared the last curtain of vines, they could see the waterfall directly ahead of them. It was about thirty feet tall and had vines and moss growing alongside it on the mountain. Along the sides of the waterfall and the banks of the river, where the cascading water landed, the rocks were glittering and reflecting multiple colors, which made it look even more beautiful than they had imagined. At the base of the waterfall was a circular pool that had been formed from the pressure of the falling water. The boys knew this would be a perfect spot for a swim.

"All I can say is WOW!" Ryan said as he started to walk down the slope toward the waterfall.

Ryan stood on the bank of the river and dipped his feet into the small circular pool that had formed near the cascading waterfall. He took off his shirt and shoes and then proceeded to dunk his whole body in the cool water. It felt so refreshing. It was deep enough to feel like he was actually somewhat clean for the first time in many days. In the heat of the jungle, he knew it wouldn't take long for his clothes to dry out once the refreshing bath was over.

Matthew started walking toward the circular pool but looked around cautiously before he made the decision to jump in. He could tell that the water was deep enough as Ryan was actually swimming and treading water. The water was calm, unlike the ocean waves they had tackled several days ago. It seemed safe enough. He was now eager to jump into the refreshing water.

Matthew took his shirt and shoes off and set his backpack next to Ryan's on the shore. He took a few steps back and then cannonballed right next to Ryan. The big splash sent a wave of water over Ryan's head, and Matthew roared with laughter. The water was so cool and refreshing. The boys continued to swim in the small circular pool that had been created by the waterfall. After splashing and playing around in the water for a while, they could feel their energy start to drain. They motioned for each other to swim over to the rock ledge under the waterfall.

They climbed up onto the rocks and let the water spray down on them as they looked at each other and smiled. It felt so good to just sit for a moment and enjoy the refreshing shower. As they sat there, they each looked around and wondered what the next step would be. Should they keep moving forward? They knew they couldn't stay here for long, but they also didn't know where they were supposed to go from here because it seemed like this was a dead end being blocked by the waterfall.

Maybe they had taken the wrong turn. Maybe they should have gone left or even straight. At least they had a moment of enjoyment at the waterfall. It seemed like it was worth the effort to get there. The boys scanned the water for fish, but they did not see anything that would provide them some supper. It had been several days now without real food, and although the fresh water was nice, it would feel so good to have something solid in their empty stomachs.

Matthew made the first move and said, "Hey, I think we should swim back over to the riverbank and lay our stuff out to dry. Then we should start thinking about moving on."

"Yeah. But where will we go? I don't see any way around this waterfall, and we certainly can't climb the mountain where the water is coming from," Ryan said as he picked up a rock and chucked it into the water, hoping for a record-breaking skip.

"Well, since we both smell a little better now, let's swim back to the riverbank and dry out a bit. Then we can go explore and try to find somewhere to settle in for the night. It will be getting dark by that time," Matthew responded as he slipped back into the cool water.

Ryan followed and began to swim to catch up to Matthew. They took a quick detour and found enough energy to dunk each other a few more times in the water before they started to swim back to the riverbank where they had left their shirts, shoes, and backpacks.

As they began to swim back, Matthew suddenly felt a tugging sensation on his legs and hollered out to Ryan, "Hey! Did you feel that? It feels like the water is pulling me toward the waterfall!"

Ryan could feel it too. It felt like a slight tug on his legs, but he kept swimming toward the shore. He didn't know what it was, but he wasn't about to waste any time trying to figure it out. He knew they needed to get back to the riverbank, and fast!

Matthew and Ryan both swam as hard and as fast as they could to get to the riverbank. As they got closer, they could feel the resistance starting to press against their bodies. They reached up to grab the rocks along the riverbank and tried to pull themselves out of the water. The current was picking up and the tugging they originally felt on their legs had now extended up their bodies. They were being sucked in!

Matthew hollered for Ryan to grab his shirt, shoes, and backpack as he did the same. They didn't know what was about to happen, but no matter what, they both knew they could not leave their backpacks behind. Their supplies had been a lifesaver; nothing was going to stop them from getting to their backpacks.

Just as both of the boys grabbed their shirts, shoes, and backpacks, they could feel the current sucking them back toward the waterfall. They were too scared to even scream. They both took a big breath, closed their eyes, and within seconds, the current sucked them down under the waterfall and everything went black.

CHAPTER

"What just happened?" Ryan said as he sat up and looked around.

What he saw shocked and terrified him at the same time. The boys were no longer in the jungle. It looked like they were in a prairie. Ryan was so shocked, he slapped himself in the face just to make sure he wasn't dreaming.

Ryan shook his head, rubbed his eyes, and then looked around again, and indeed, they were still in the prairie. They were lying next to a small stream where they must have come from. He saw Matthew still lying next to him, and he crawled over to give him a shove. Matthew wasn't moving yet, but he could see him breathing, so he knew he must be okay. *Boy, would he be surprised when he woke up,* Ryan thought to himself as he started to look around for the backpacks, shirts, and shoes, hoping desperately everything had arrived with them.

Ryan waited longer for Matthew to wake up, but when he didn't, Ryan pulled the same move on him Matthew had the first day they landed on the beach. He rolled Matthew over and smacked him across the face. Matthew sprung up and threw his hands up as if to defend himself against whatever it was that was attacking him.

Matthew quickly realized it was Ryan who had slapped him and he put his arms down, but gave him a stern look and said, "Uh, what happened? Where are we?"

Ryan eagerly responded, "It was like we were flushed down a toilet and ended up in the sewer. Except instead of a sewer, we landed in a prairie!" Ryan quickly added, "Thank God it wasn't the sewer!"

They both remembered being in the small pond and the current picking up and sucking them down under the waterfall. But, how did they get here? And where was here? Were they still on the same island? Who or what transported them?

"So, why do you suppose we are now in a prairie? Is this still part of this mysterious game we are supposed to be playing?" Matthew asked Ryan, as if Ryan was supposed to know the answers to all his questions.

Ryan just shrugged. He had located the backpacks and most of the supplies had been strewn out all over the grass. It was definitely a different world where they were now. He gathered up all the supplies and the backpacks and brought them back over to where Matthew was still sitting. The boys loaded their supplies back into their backpacks, put their shoes and shirts on, and then took a moment to look around at their new surroundings.

In the distance, they saw the same volcano they had seen when they arrived on the island, so they determined they were still on the same island, just in a different area. As they continued to look around, they started to discuss the journey they had been on and began to retrace the challenges they had faced.

Ryan recalled, "Each time we completed a challenge together using teamwork, we were rewarded with food and water, and of course, our supplies to survive."

"Yeah, and as our challenges moved from the beach and boat to the jungle, every time we encountered a challenge there was some kind of circular thing in our path – like the platform next to the temple and the waterfall pool," Matthew responded as if he was attempting to connect the dots.

Ryan took a moment to think and then responded, "Then there was that key you found in the chest in the temple. Even though the web of vines wasn't perfectly round, the chest was directly in the center of the temple. Maybe we need to be looking for keys and round things? Not sure what they mean, but maybe they are clues to help us get off this mysterious island?"

Matthew took out his key and looked at it again as he pondered what Ryan had said and after several minutes he replied, "Well, obviously a key is used to either lock or unlock something. Now that you mention it, we've always found either food and water, the key, or the way to the next part of the island in the center of the circle. I think we are onto something now!"

"Okay, Captain Obvious! So, let's assume this is a game, right? Well, the gamekeepers must have a plan, but we have to be willing to move forward, look for the clues, and take on the challenges to get to the next step in the game," Ryan said as he practically finished Matthew's thought for him.

Matthew flashed a big grin and said, "It's kinda like being in the eye of a storm. The place where there is calm while everything else is flying around out of control. We need to focus on being in the eye of the storm!"

Matthew again recalled what his parents had described as being a wizard, the balance to the warrior. He always felt like they were lecturing him when he was complaining about the challenges he faced at school or in sports. He remembered them saying things like, "Focus on what you want and not on what you don't want; create clear intentions and commit to them." The one he was now remembering the most was, "I am the eye of the storm; I stay calm and centered regardless of anything."

Boy was this the right time to remember these things, Matthew thought to himself as he now realized how much his parents were trying to help him get through those tough times. He missed them so much now and just wanted to go home. He knew he had to find a way back to them. He would do anything in his power to make that happen.

Although the boys didn't have all the answers yet, they knew they had to be onto something, and if they remained focused on moving forward and trying to find the "eye of the storm" along their journey, before long, they would conquer the game and find a way off the island. With renewed encouragement and energy, they continued to talk and assess their surroundings while they rested a bit longer on the edge of the stream that had brought them into the prairie.

Matthew began to repack his key into his backpack. When he looked up, he spotted something in the distance and said, "Ryan, is that a fire over there? Could it be a campfire? Do you think someone else is here with us?"

"No! That fire is definitely not a campfire. It's huge!" Ryan said as he jumped up to take a better look at the fire looming in the distance.

The boys quickly realized they were in big trouble once again. They scrambled to gather up their supplies and loaded them as fast as they could into their backpacks. Before long, the fire had grown rapidly and was coming right toward them! They looked around to see if there was any water near them to put out the fire.

They knew that even the small stream they had come out of was too small to put this kind of fire out, and all they had were two small cups, so that wouldn't work. As they continued to search for a larger water source, it began to rain. The rain, however, didn't seem like ordinary rain. It smelled like lighter fluid. In fact, it was lighter fluid! Everything was being doused by lighter fluid; within minutes, the fire would be right on top of them.

With desperation in his eyes, Ryan ran over to the stream. He had to find a way to get the water out of the stream to flow into the prairie and saturate the grass in front of them. It was a long shot, but it was their only hope. He started lifting the rocks away from the banks of the small stream and tossed them away from the sides of the bank, as deep as they could, into the prairie. Matthew didn't know what he was doing but started to help Ryan anyway.

As they removed the last rock from the bank of the stream, water suddenly started to flow down into the prairie and soon, the ground around them was completely saturated. The wall of water was enough to provide a barricade from the fire. Soon the lighter fluid rain dissipated and the prairie grass began to smolder as the fire hit the saturated ground in front of the boys.

After the short battle, and thanks to the quick thinking of

Ryan, the boys fell down onto the soggy ground and both exhaled a sigh of relief. They had conquered another challenge using their teamwork and strong will. As they sat there, they looked off into the distance where the fire had started, and they couldn't believe what they were now seeing. Had it been there the entire time and the fire was just blocking it? Or, did it just appear once they put the fire out?

What they saw was a circular platform coming out of the ground in the distance. It appeared to be right where the fire started. They knew they had to get to the platform, but needed to wait for the scorched prairie grass to finish smoldering. As they waited, they worked through their strategy.

"I think we should just run full out and jump onto the platform and tackle whatever might be lurking on top of it," Ryan said as he continued to examine the platform from afar.

Matthew rolled his eyes and said, "Of course, that doesn't surprise me! I think we should be more cautious and go around the back side over by the grove of trees over there. Then we can see what might be waiting for us because this is guaranteed to be a trap of some sort."

"Well, it won't do us any good to frolic through the prairie. Get your knife out and get ready because we are moving on the count of three," Ryan declared as he jumped up and got into racing position.

Ryan counted to three and was then off like a bullet. He started running as fast as he could toward the platform; Matthew took off after him. As they sprinted across the prairie toward the platform, the boys imagined all the possibilities of what was in store for them. As they approached the platform, they slowed their pace and came to a stop at the edge of the platform. It was then they saw food packets, water, and a small key made of stone lying in the center of the platform. It was just as they had been talking about prior to the prairie fire.

The key wasn't quite what they had expected since they already had one mystery key they didn't know what to do with, but they knew they desperately needed more food and water. They would eventually figure out what to do with the key. As they stepped up toward the platform to reach for the treasures in the center, it rose up out of the ground further just beyond their reach. They jumped up to grab the items in the center and it rose again. The boys looked at each other confused and frustrated. They stood there for a moment and brainstormed what to do to get the food and the key.

This time, Matthew came up with the plan. He grabbed Ryan's backpack and pulled out the rope. He then looked for a big rock. He wrapped the rope around the rock and secured it as tight as he could with a thick knot. He took his new weapon and started to swing it around in circles over his head, like a cowboy trying to lasso a steer.

He tossed it toward the platform, hoping to land the rock close to the supplies and then pull the supplies off the platform with the weight of the heavy rock. It took a couple of tries, but when he tossed it on the third try, the rock landed just where he was hoping. He yanked on the rope and down came the food, water, and the key followed by the big rock.

"Yes! We got it. Finally!" Ryan yelled as he grabbed the food packets, water, and the key off the ground. Ryan examined the stone key and was about to stuff it into his backpack when he saw Matthew giving him an evil glare. Ryan had no idea what he had done wrong, but instead of shoving it into his backpack, he handed the key over to Matthew, who apparently wanted to take a look too.

"What do you think these keys are for?" Matthew said as he examined the key.

"Well, the wooden box idea is out because there are two keys now instead of one and both couldn't be for the wooden box. Maybe we just need to hold on to them for something later, because I can't see a need for them now...Unless there is a mansion for each of us up ahead in that grove of trees and those keys open the doors!" Ryan responded with a new wave of excitement in his voice.

Once again, Matthew found himself rolling his eyes at his best friend. After all they had gone through, did Ryan really think there was a mansion in their future? Matthew was simply hoping for some shelter under the trees. Matthew continued to examine both of the keys more carefully, and he noticed something they had in common. Both keys had the exact same teeth pattern on them. They were essentially the same key that should fit into the same key hole, but made of different material.

Now Matthew was even more confused. He stacked both keys together, one on top of the other, and carefully placed them into his backpack. Whatever the reason was that they were given these keys, he wanted to ensure he had them ready when the time came. In fact, they very well could be their ticket off the island. Although, he secretly did like Ryan's idea that the grand prize was a mansion for each of them just beyond the grove of trees ahead.

"Well, I think we should get a move on to see where we end up next. Hopefully, it's a colder climate because I'm starting to get hot. Oh wait. I already was!" Ryan said as he laughed and started strutting like he was modeling clothes on a runway.

"Okay, Mr. Creepy! You can stop walking like that now or I might puke!" Matthew declared as he grinned and turned his head to the side, faking he was about to throw up.

Matthew was also hoping for a colder climate so he could cool off. Although the prairie was less humid and there was a slight breeze helping a little, the temperature was still very warm and the energy they were expending through all these challenges kept their body temp even higher than it would normally be.

The boys walked, with Ryan just a little further ahead of Matthew, as he continued to demonstrate his catwalk on the runway of the prairie. Ryan would periodically turn around and flash a grin, just checking to make sure Matthew was still admiring the view.

They walked toward the grove of trees they had seen in the distance, but they really didn't know where they were going or what they could expect to find in the trees. The burned prairie grass crunched under their feet as they got closer and closer to the trees. All of a sudden, Ryan disappeared deep into the ground!

CHAPTER

Matthew ran ahead trying to see where Ryan had gone, and he came to a screeching halt at the edge of a huge pit in the ground. Ryan had fallen into the pit, which was covered up by what looked like burned prairie grass. It must have been a trap. Someone again had set this trap likely hoping both would end up inside, and if they had, they would have been doomed for sure. *Who was behind all of this?* Matthew thought to himself as he quickly thanked God that he had not fallen in along with Ryan.

Matthew hollered down into the pit and asked, "Ryan! Are you okay?"

Ryan responded from the depths of the dark pit, "Um, yep, I think so."

Ryan was examining his arms and legs to make sure nothing was broken after he fell into the hole. If he had broken anything, they would really be in serious trouble. If he wasn't able to walk, how would they ever make it off the island? Ryan reached down with his arms to push himself up to a stand. When he did, he felt a sharp pain in his butt. He wondered if he had broken his tailbone when he fell. It was an awful pain, and he hoped he didn't break it because sitting and walking were going to be really hard from here on out, let alone running and jumping, like all the other obstacles required so far.

"Hey! Are you okay? Are you hurt?" Matthew hollered again down into the dark hole.

Ryan stood up and responded, "Yeah! I'm fine. My butt really hurts though. I think I might have broken my tailbone, or at least I've got one nasty bruised butt."

"Serves you right for shaking it in front of me for the past half hour," Matthew shouted down at Ryan, trying to lighten the mood a bit.

Ryan was definitely not in the mood for jokes and just wanted to figure out a way to get out of the nasty dark pit. It was so dark and cold, he couldn't see anything around him, and he didn't even want to imagine what might be crawling inside the earth around him. The pit seemed to be about twenty feet deep. He thought about trying to climb up the side of the pit, but it was too wide and the earthen walls were too hard and slippery for his hands and feet to get any traction.

Matthew hollered down again, seeing that Ryan's efforts to climb out were useless, "Maybe if I throw down the rope, I can pull you up."

Matthew was thankful he had stuffed the rope into his own backpack after they captured the treasures on the platform in the prairie. He dug through his backpack and grabbed the rope. As he thought about his plan for a bit longer, he knew he would not have enough strength to pull Ryan up on his own. He recalled the near-catastrophic disaster they faced when he was trying to rescue Ryan from falling down into the deep chasm at the site of the temple.

It was the tree root that saved them both. That was it! He needed to secure the rope around something steady and strong like a tree. Then Ryan could climb while Matthew pulled, and before long, he should be out of the pit. Matthew looked around at the grove of trees and spotted the closest one he thought would be strong enough to hold Ryan.

He grabbed the rope, ran over to the tree, and tied the rope around the base. Then he ran back to the pit where he could see Ryan standing, looking up at him, desperately wanting out. It was as if Ryan was in prison and Matthew was bringing him bread and water. Matthew glanced at his watch and knew he needed to get Ryan out of the pit soon, as the sun would be setting and spending the night in the pit and being exposed to the elements and creatures of the prairie was not Matthew's idea of a good time.

Matthew tossed the rope and hollered down to Ryan, "I've got the rope secured to a tree. Take the rope, secure it around your waist, and start climbing. On your count, I'm going to pull while you climb."

Matthew picked a spot far enough away from the edge of the pit to avoid being pulled in by the weight of Ryan, and then he sat on the ground. He dug his heels into the charred prairie ground and he heard Ryan do his count. The tension increased on the rope and Matthew pulled with every ounce of strength he had left in his body.

Matthew could hear Ryan grunting and occasionally screaming out in pain, declaring how bad his butt hurt from the effort he was making to get out of the pit. All they could do now was continue to climb and pull, climb and pull, and repeat until Ryan cleared the edge of the pit. After several minutes, Ryan had finally reached the surface.

Ryan flung his right leg over the edge of the pit and Matthew gave one final tug. Both of the boys went flying backward, landing on their backs. They lay there silent for several minutes on the crisp prairie ground as they breathed heavily in and out. Matthew finally raised his arms up over his head in an attempt to let as much air into his lungs as possible, while Ryan rolled onto his side and reached down to hold his sore butt.

As their gasping for air subsided, Matthew pushed himself up to a sitting position and locked his arms around his knees to steady himself. Ryan propped himself up onto his side as he didn't dare put any pressure on his butt. The boys scanned the prairie and suddenly realized how exposed they really were out there. Although they were close to the grove of trees along the edge of the prairie, they knew they needed to get into the cluster of trees to protect themselves from whatever might be lurking in the prairie.

"We better get moving," Matthew said as he saw Ryan drop his arm that he was propped up on and roll back onto his side.

Ryan let out a moan and responded, "But my butt! It hurts so bad I don't want to move. I'm exhausted."

Matthew couldn't imagine how bad it must have hurt to have fallen down into that pit, and he recognized how exhausted they both were from the rescue effort, so he backed off and let Ryan rest for a few more moments. Ryan was really in a lot of pain and looked like he was going to throw up. They certainly didn't need that to deal with that along with all of the other challenges they were facing.

Several more minutes went by, and Matthew nudged Ryan and finally said, "Okay. We need to get moving so we don't get eaten."

The boys stood up and started walking toward the grove of trees that would be their home for the night. Ryan limped in pain and swore to Matthew that he would never shake his butt at him again. As they neared the trees, they noticed a very peculiar thing. The grove of trees formed a circle, and there was apparently only one way in and one way out.

"That's strange, don't you think?" Ryan said as they got closer to the circular grove of trees.

Matthew looked around and although this was exactly what they had been talking about with finding circular areas within the prairie, he couldn't help but wonder what kind of trap they were getting themselves into again. They continued to move forward, and just as they reached the entrance of the trees, they saw an object glinting in the sunlight directly in the center of the circle of trees. It looked like the handle of a knife sticking halfway out of the ground.

"Hey! Do you see that over there? It looks like a knife sticking out of the ground," Matthew said as he started walking a little faster toward where the object was buried.

"It's about time something good happens for us. I was hoping there would have been another knife granted to us on the platform back there, but now here it is," Ryan exclaimed with excitement.

Matthew bent down to pull the knife out of the ground and

said, "I wouldn't get too excited Ryan. This likely means that we are going to be needing this sometime soon."

"Oh, yeah. I guess I never thought about it that way," Ryan said as he reached out to take the knife from Matthew's hands.

Ryan turned it over and examined it from every angle. It looked just like the one they had gotten from the boat. The one Matthew had been carrying. The one that saved them from his "girlfriend" in the jungle. Ryan didn't know what was about to happen, but he felt relieved he too would now have a knife to carry.

While Ryan was examining the knife and shining it up with his shirt, Matthew explored the circular boundary of the trees. Other than the fact the trees were in a perfect circle, nothing looked unusual. He picked a tree and plopped himself down underneath it, resting his back against the bark.

Matthew called out to his buddy, "Come on, Ryan. It's already been a long enough day, and we need to get some food and water in us. Quit kissing your knife and let's eat."

"Right on!" Ryan said, as he was happy to eat any time he heard the dinner bell ring, even if it was only the food packets and water that were being served.

The boys sat happily under the trees indulging in their food packets and drinking their water. It felt so good to be resting, if only for a moment. Ryan continued to shift his weight as he sat under the tree. Although the pain in his tailbone had gotten better, it was still there, reminding him of the fall he had taken into the depths of the pit. That experience would definitely remain fresh in his mind as a reminder to always watch for unexpected traps along the journey they were on.

When he couldn't sit any longer, Ryan stood up and said, "I'm going to get us some branches so we can start a fire tonight. It's already starting to cool down, and I don't want to have to curl up next to you to stay warm tonight."

"Maybe your 'girlfriend' will come back for you to help you stay warm," Matthew responded sarcastically.

Just as Matthew finished his comment, the boys heard a rustling in the trees surrounding them. Matthew jumped to his feet and grabbed his knife. Ryan quickly pulled his knife out of the ground by the tree where he had been sitting. All of a sudden, the boys had several pairs of eyes glowing at them from in between the trees.

"I think I spoke too soon," Matthew said as he and Ryan stood back to back in the center of the circle of trees.

"Yeah! It looks like my 'girlfriend' is back and she brought some friends for you!" Ryan said as he clutched his knife tighter in his hand.

Just as Ryan finished his statement, the beasts jumped out from behind the trees and surrounded Matthew and Ryan. These beasts looked just like the ones in the jungle, only this time they had multiplied! Without speaking a word, the boys raised their fists with their knives clutched tightly and started to attack.

They knew they needed to get the beasts to rear up so they could stab them in the chest. They each took a low swipe with their knives across the beasts' front legs, and that was enough to make them really, really angry. They reared up and the boys reached up with their knives and stabbed the beasts in the center of their chests. They ducked to avoid the beasts falling on top of them, but before they could, the beasts disappeared, just like the first one they had encountered in the jungle.

The next round of beasts came after them, and the boys continued to fight. With each swing, they felt more confidence rising within them, and soon they were fighting more than one at a time. They lost track of the number they fought, but it had to have been at least seven. They remained physically positioned in the center of the circle of trees, and despite the battle they were facing with so many beasts coming at them from every angle, they remained centered and focused on the challenge.

They now knew what it was like to be in the eye of the storm. The boys realized they were stronger and braver than they thought they were, and they knew from that moment on, they would be approaching this game differently. They would not be facing the challenges on the island just to survive. This game was now theirs to win!

As the last beast disappeared and the green goo dried up, the boys sat down in the center of the circle of trees and breathed a sigh of relief. They sat there for a moment, resting back to back and feeling the support they had in each other. Ryan had completely forgotten already about the pain in his butt and Matthew had forgotten about how tired he was from another long and strenuous day.

It was as if time stood still and the boys just sat and savored the moment of their victory. They were again so grateful they had each other and that they were able to overcome yet another challenge.

Finally, Ryan spoke first, "That was so scary I almost peed my pants again! I thought we were dead."

Matthew chuckled and said, "Yep, I'm with you on that one.

I'm a little disappointed though that your 'girlfriend's' friends weren't any better looking than she was!"

"Ha! Ha!" Ryan said as he stood up and made his way back toward the tree where they had left their backpacks.

He felt he had had enough of this bonding time with his best friend and decided to continue his quest to gather some branches and light the campfire. It was now darker and was becoming diffcult to see, so he knew he couldn't wait any longer. He gathered enough branches to get a small fire started, enough to provide ample light and a little heat to keep them warm from the cool night air.

The boys both gathered some more branches and piled them onto the fire while they laid out their blankets and got ready for another much-needed night of rest. As they got situated, they talked about their adventures and laughed at the sheer madness of it all. They felt relieved they had made it through another day and were anticipating what would lie ahead for them tomorrow. They expected more "opportunities" to come their way, but they were starting to feel more prepared now to handle whatever they would be required to face.

Just as they were about to drift off to sleep, Ryan let out a quiet laugh and said, "Hey, remember when you were chopping vines in the jungle and the moss fell all over you? That was so hilarious. You looked like you turned into a green one of those beasts."

"Yeah, well at least I didn't pee my pants. Get wrecked!" Matthew jeered as he gave him a taunting look and laughed at him.

Ryan rolled over and ignored Matthew's comment. Within minutes, both of the boys had drifted off to sleep…

CHAPTER 14

In the morning, the boys awoke as the sun glinted across their eyes. Reggie crowed and startled them awake. This time, thankfully, there was no ugly beast breathing on their faces, but all they could think about was sleeping longer. It had been a rough few days, and despite the good sleep they had gotten, they were still exhausted.

Reggie continued to crow until both boys were awake. It was as if Reggie knew they would have slept all day if they could. They sat up and rubbed their eyes, wishing that when they had opened them, they had been magically transported back to wherever it was they came from before they were placed on this island.

"Uh, why can't we sleep for five more minutes, Reggie? Do you have to wake us up so early?" Ryan groaned as he sat up.

Ryan wondered how it was possible they were now in a different climate, on a different part of the island, and maybe even in a different world, yet that darn rooster continued to find them! He envisioned stabbing the bird with his new knife and cooking it over a hot campfire. Not only would he have the pleasure of real food in his stomach, but he wouldn't have to hear Reggie's annoying cock-a-doodle-doo every morning.

"Dude, I agree with you, what is up with that thing? Why can't he crow a little bit later so we can sleep longer, or at least stop like a normal rooster would do?" Matthew said as he sat up and continued his protest as he yelled to the bird, "Hey! Shut up, you dumb bird!"

Now that Reggie had completed the job and the boys were offcially awake, they gathered up their supplies and put them in their backpacks. They ate their last food packet and drank another bottle of water. Now, each time they ate, they appreciated the fact it could very well be their last meal and they no longer took the meals for granted. They knew they had to get moving this morning so they could go explore the prairie. They both were eager to see if they could find any real food and some more water somewhere.

"Let's bring our backpacks and go look for some food and water, and maybe a way off this island," Ryan said as he looked beyond the circle of trees they had slept in for the night.

"Yeah. I agree, let's get going. It feels like this place is a death trap, like we are sitting ducks waiting for something to come and attack us. Let's go before we get eaten. I don't think that would feel very good," Matthew said as he packed up his belongings.

Ryan pointed to the area where the boys had entered the circle of trees and said, "Let's head back that way and see if we can follow that stream we were lying next to when we entered the prairie. If we don't find anything on our exploration today, we can at least follow it back to this grove of trees since we would at least have shelter here again for another night. Who knows what we will find out there in the prairie today."

Both boys grabbed their backpacks and headed out. They hadn't gone far before they reached the small stream. They saw the rocks they had cleared away from the banks of the stream. Somehow, despite the rocks being strewn all over the prairie, the water had receded back into the stream. They followed the stream for several miles before they saw anything that caught their attention. They were appreciative of the fact they had not encountered any more of those ugly beasts, and they were even more excited when they saw a group of small fruit trees growing alongside the stream.

The fruit looked delicious, plump, and juicy. It appeared to be plums, with a brilliant purple color, and it was the most amazing thing the boys had seen in several days. It was almost like Christmas morning with beautiful ornaments hanging on the tree, only these were edible. Both boys wanted to devour the entire tree without even wasting time to pick the fruit off!

"Dude! A fruit tree. It looks so good!" Ryan exclaimed as he looked at it with extreme desire.

Ryan went over and picked one of the fresh plums off the tree and sunk his teeth deep into the plump fruit. The fruit burst with flavor in his mouth. The juice flowed down the sides of his mouth and onto his shirt. Ryan wiped his mouth with the back of his arm and continued to sink his teeth in for another bite. He could literally feel the pulp of the fruit and the juice sink deep into his belly. It was an amazing feeling to finally have something to fill his stomach.

"Hey! Leave some for me. Don't eat them all," Matthew said as he rushed over and plucked the fruit off the branch.

"What do you think these are?" Ryan asked with a mouth full of fruit, barely articulate enough to understand.

Matthew took another bite, enjoyed the sweet sensation, and replied, "I have no idea. At first, I thought they might be kinda like plums, but they taste bitter and are less juicy than plums. I really don't think we need to worry about naming them anyway, the way you are slamming them down. By the time we think of a name, they will all be gone."

"Well, nobody is stopping you from doing the same, so try to keep up if you can," Ryan responded as he grabbed another fruit off the tree.

Both boys continued to eat, and as they chomped on one piece of fruit, they picked another and loaded up their backpacks. Before long, there was no room left and they had to pull their empty water bottles out of their backpacks to make room for a few extra pieces of fruit. Each of the backpacks was heavily weighted down now, and all they needed was some water to wash down their flavorful meal.

Their bellies were filled to the brim, and they could hardly even bend over to gather up the empty water bottles. As they did, they could feel the fruit sliding to the top of their backpacks and then back down again as they stood up. It was a great feeling to know they had some food at least for the next few days before it would likely spoil.

Matthew ran over to the stream, bent down and cupped his hands to capture some of the cold, refreshing water. He took a small taste and believed it was clean, so he scooped up a few more handfuls before he opened the empty water bottles and filled them with the cold water from the stream. He filled each bottle to the very top and then closed the cap. He repeated this process with Ryan's water bottles and then stood up.

Ryan was standing over him, still licking his lips and cheeks from all the juice that remained on his face from the fruit, and he said, "I wish I was a camel. They can go days without water. We can only go four days, and with these challenges we have faced, I don't think we could even travel after two days."

"Um, okay. That was a weird teaching moment. Thanks for sharing, but I honestly don't care about how long camels can go without water. All I care about is how to transport our water from one place to another and about how much water we have left," Matthew said, wondering where his friend came up with his random comments.

Ryan finally stopped licking his lips and bent down by the stream to collect a few handfuls of water and said, "Jeez! Just saying."

As the boys finished collecting their water and gathering the bottles into their arms, they stood and looked around. There was absolutely nothing out there in the open prairie. The stream and fruit tree were the only things that seemed to have any glimmer of life. A sense of dread began to overcome the boys. Would this be the end for them? It didn't seem like there was any way off this prairie. It felt as if they could literally walk for miles and not get anywhere.

Ryan looked at Matthew with a funny look on his face and said, "I think we should just head back to the grove of trees, back up the stream. I'm not feeling very well all of a sudden."

Matthew saw Ryan turning a bit pale and figured he was just nauseous from gorging himself with all the fruit. He looked back at the stream they had traveled along to reach the fruit tree and thought it was a safe bet to just head back to the circle of trees where they had found shelter the night before. He was hopeful the beasts would not return and they could enjoy another round of fruit before they went to sleep. He figured they could both use some additional rest anyway. As he was pondering his plan, Matthew started to have a wave of nausea come over him. It must have been what Ryan had been trying to describe.

Matthew looked at Ryan and said, "I'm starting to feel sick now too. Let's head back before it's too late."

"Too late? Do you think that fruit was poisonous or something?" Ryan said with a look of fear coming over his pale face.

"I think we just ate too much and now we are paying the price. Let's go," Matthew said as another wave of nausea hit him in the center of his gut.

Matthew didn't know what was going on, but he felt a sudden urge to get back to the grove of trees, the safest spot he knew so far on the prairie. The boys followed the stream back. As they got closer to the grove of trees, their legs started to feel like heavy logs of cement. They could hardly move and had to drag themselves along. Between the weight of the fruit in their backpacks, the heavy water bottles in their arms, and now the feeling of concrete legs, they were not sure if they could continue.

Ryan saw the entrance to the circle of trees and said weakly, "There it is."

Ryan turned to head toward the area they had exited from that morning and Matthew followed. Both were now literally dragging themselves into the shelter of the trees. They made their way to the center where they had so bravely fought off the beasts the night before. As they reached the center, they collapsed with exhaustion onto the hard ground.

They lay there facing each other and could feel themselves drifting in and out of consciousness. The waves of nausea continued, and extreme fatigue overcame their bodies. They tried to move, but their effort was futile. Their bodies were now in a state of paralysis. Moments later, they felt the circle of trees close around them, and felt everything around them spinning out of control, as if they were in the eye of a tornado.

The speed of the rotation increased rapidly and they could feel themselves being sucked into the center of the earth…within seconds, they were gone!

CHAPTER

The boys woke up with their faces planted in the sand. They rolled onto their backs and were blinded by the hot scorching sun beating down on them. They could not see a thing. All they knew was they were both there. Somehow they had made it to wherever they were, together. At first, they thought they were back on the shore where they had started this horrific journey, but this time something felt different.

Matthew was the first to sit up. He squinted and shielded his eyes with this hand in an attempt to get a better look around. Ryan spit the sand out of his mouth that he had ingested with his face plant, and then proceeded to follow Matthew in the process of scanning the area around them.

Where were they now?

The last thing they remembered was making it back to the circular grove of trees, and the next thing they knew, they were waking up with faces buried in the sand. The temperature was scorching hot and the sand was so fine. The wind had whipped up a sand wall next to where they were lying, and that appeared to be the only shelter they had around them. They finally realized where they were...

They were in the desert!

"I thought I asked for a cooler climate!" Ryan said as he started to dig the sand out of his ears and nose.

"Seriously, dude! It's bad enough we are in this place, but watching you pick your nose is the last thing I wanted to wake up to. I would rather have another morning encounter with your 'girlfriend' than see you do that again!" Matthew declared as he turned away in disgust.

"Okay! Okay! I see your point, but I had to get it out somehow. I didn't figure you would help me or that we would be finding a shower anytime soon," Ryan responded as he scowled back at his best friend and then promptly stuck his tongue out at Matthew.

The boys continued to evaluate their surroundings. They saw the volcano looming in the distance, so they knew they were still on the island, just in a different area again. This time, it appeared they were in the desert as there was sand and sand dunes as far as they could see. Ryan began to look further ahead, and off in the opposite direction of where they had seen the volcano he spotted something, but couldn't quite make out what it was. The wind was blowing the sand around, and with the sun beating down on them, it was hard to see anything clearly. However, Ryan knew he had seen something beyond the immediate area where they had landed.

Ryan gazed off into the distance and then pointed toward the area he had first seen the object and said, "Hey, Matthew, I think I see something just beyond that sand dune over there."

Matthew strained to see but was not able to identify anything other than a large sand dune directly ahead of them. In fact, there were sand dunes all around them. There was nothing but sand in this barren desert they were now in. But, maybe there was something over there. Maybe Ryan had spotted something?

It didn't look like there was any shelter anywhere near them, and although the area Ryan had been pointing to looked pretty far away, the boys knew from their past experiences on the island they needed to continue to press on despite their fear and the uncertainty of what may lie ahead.

"Let's go check it out. Maybe there will be something useful over there and hopefully, another clue to find a way off this strange island," Matthew said as he started to look around for his backpack.

Ryan was hunting for the same thing and responded, "Yeah. It kinda feels like we are a broken record now. We keep saying the same thing over and over. We want some food and water and a way off this stupid island. Repeat times one million."

They continued to search for their backpacks, as they knew they would not survive long out in the middle of the desert without their supplies and some water. Even with the water they had collected on the prairie, they knew they would need to find some additional water out there. If they did, they might be in good shape for the rest of their journey, but if there wasn't any water, the boys wouldn't have a chance of surviving this climate, let alone getting off the island.

The hunt for the backpacks continued. As it turned into a longer search, the boys became more concerned by the minute that somehow their backpacks didn't make it along for the ride to the desert. They frantically started digging in the sand near where they had landed and finally, they struck gold! They were anticipating the fresh fruit they had picked, until they remembered the fruit must have been what poisoned them and caused them to lose consciousness back on the prairie.

Matthew pulled his backpack out of the sand and it was considerably lighter than it had been the last time he remembered it. He unzipped the backpack and only the supplies were there. There was no fruit and no water bottles. Ryan saw Matthew's expression, and the empty backpack, and dug more aggressively in the sand hoping his would be filled with at least the water bottles. Finally, he found his too. Unfortunately, the results were the same. Not only was he missing the fruit he had loaded into the backpack, there were no water bottles, and the knife he found in the prairie was gone too.

Matthew had been looking over his shoulder as Ryan dug through his backpack. After seeing the empty bag, Matthew was devastated and dropped to his knees in the hot sand. What were they going to do without their water? The fruit they had eaten had obviously been tainted, so they could do without the fruit, but they definitely needed the water to survive.

It was already so hot out in the desert, and they could hardly see anything. They had no sense of direction and all they were doing was taking a risk by setting off on yet another journey. Although they knew the risk, they couldn't think of any alternative other than to die trying to find their way out of this challenge.

Ryan pulled Matthew up off his knees in the sand and they rolled up their pant legs and then took off their shirts and wrapped them around their heads. They thought they remembered seeing this somewhere before and thought it not only looked cool, but it might be just enough to prevent the sun from scorching their heads along the way. They would need to do everything they could to stay cool and hydrated.

The boys gathered up their backpacks and finally set off on the path toward the object Ryan had seen in the distance. They hiked through the desert for several hours, but despite their effort, it felt as if they were literally standing in place. Nothing seemed to change in their surroundings except for the temperature getting hotter and hotter. It was as if someone kept turning up the heat in the oven.

Not only was the temperature rising, but they started to notice the sand dune they were trudging on felt like it was getting bigger and bigger. Every step they took, the boys became even more exhausted. When they first set out toward the sand dune to locate the object Ryan had seen in the distance, they knew they would be traveling some distance, but it was almost as if someone kept moving the sand dune further and further away from them. By this point, the boys had lost all sense of where they were until Ryan located something different in the distance.

"Hey, I see some small cacti growing in the valley between those two sand dunes over there," Ryan said as he stopped in his tracks and pointed at an area just beyond the peak of the sand dune where they were presently standing.

"Yeah. I see it too this time," Matthew said almost as if he needed to reassure himself of what he was seeing.

Ryan started on another one of his scientific educational lectures and said, "Maybe if we cut those cacti open, there will be water inside. I remember reading somewhere that sometimes cacti have water in them. If it is the right type of cactus, we can drink it without worrying about getting sick from it. Or, there may be water under the ground where there are a bunch of cacti."

Matthew was so excited he started jumping up and down and said, "Ryan, did you hear what you just said?"

Ryan looked confused and said, "Yeah, I heard what I just said, because I just said it."

"No! What you just said is that you 'remembered reading somewhere'! We just keep getting closer to having all of our memories back," Matthew said as he stopped jumping up and down and grabbed Ryan by the shoulders to recognize the moment. After a few flashbacks and memories surfacing throughout their journey, Matthew was becoming more hopeful that both of their memories would return and they would recall how they ended up on the island. If they did, perhaps they could figure out how to get off the island before it was too late.

"Okay! Okay! You are starting to creep me out again. I almost thought you were going to hug me or something. Let's go get some water because you might be losing your mind," Ryan said as he took off toward the cacti. Ryan was grateful to have remembered something, but he knew they needed water, and fast!

It was certainly a lot easier traveling down the sand dune than it was making their way up. And, as they made their way down, the temperature felt a bit cooler. The boys had hope they would be able to recover even a few drops from the cacti they had seen from the peak of the sand dune.

Ryan reached the cacti first and he knelt down and held out his hand, as if he was a surgeon asking for a scalpel. Matthew responded immediately by pulling out his knife from his backpack and handing it over to Ryan. Ryan didn't know if this was the right type of cactus to drink from, but he thought they would die either way if they didn't take the risk.

He cut off the top of the cactus and then started shaving off the prickles with the knife far enough down so he could attempt to squeeze the cactus to retrieve the pulp. He took off his shirt he had wrapped around his head and motioned for Matthew to do the same. He scooped out a glob of pulp from the cactus and placed it in the center or his shirt. He wadded it up and then wrung it out like a wet rag onto his finger. He actually got a drop out.

He carefully brought the drop that landed on his finger up to his mouth and sucked the drop of cactus juice down, dirty finger and all. As the drop touched his tongue, Ryan made the ugliest face Matthew had ever seen.

Ryan squinted, shook his head, and proceeded to stick out his tongue and yelled, "Yeeow! That is so bitter! Yuck!"

"Let me try. This is a matter of life and death, so we better figure out how to suck it up and get some of that juice in us," Matthew said like a general in command of his fleet.

Ryan gladly handed it over to Matthew. As he tasted the juice from the cactus, the same expression spread across Matthew's face. The boys looked at each other and definitely knew they needed a different plan. If they couldn't tolerate even one drop of this, there was no way they would get enough value from continuing the process since they would end up throwing up and then they would be in worse shape. They at least knew now this must not be the right kind of cactus to drink from.

Ryan put the shirt down and started to dig around the base

of the cacti where they found a slight pooling of water deep within the sand. They each placed their shirts in the small pit of water and proceeded to wring it out and catch the drops of water from the saturated shirts. After a few rounds of the process, they knew this wouldn't sustain them long and they needed to keep going. They had to be close now and they felt like they were just wasting time, when time was really running out for them.

"Let's just keep going and eventually we will get there. If we don't die first," Matthew said with frustration as he took the damp shirt and wrapped it back around his head.

"Yeah. Hopefully, we get there before dying," Ryan said sarcastically as he looked at Matthew and proceeded to do the same thing as Matthew had with his shirt.

Ryan knew Matthew was being sarcastic and that he was exhausted, but Ryan felt that neither one of them should be sending these negative intentions out into the universe. Ryan believed they should remain focused on getting to the top of the sand dune in the distance and not be thinking about dying. All it would take was focusing on one step at a time. Now Ryan was the one getting frustrated. Not the typical way it went for the two boys. It was generally Matthew who had little patience for Ryan, but now the roles were reversed.

"Sorry. I was just saying!" Matthew said as they stared at each other, frustrated not only by each other's comments but by the situation they were in again.

Both of the boys had fire in their eyes and continued to hold their ground as they glared at each other. Suddenly, they heard a loud roar coming from beyond the valley between the two sand dunes where they had discovered the cacti. That was enough to promptly end the feud for good. Both boys looked at each other, quickly grabbed their backpacks, turned around, and started running between the two sand dunes in the original direction they were heading prior to the cacti detour.

They reached the end of the valley where the two sand dunes merged, and the next battle began, to climb to the peak. The boys started climbing, and with every step, their legs burned more and more, and their throats dried to a crisp with each breath they took. Their bodies and their mouths were begging for water the entire way up. Finally, they reached the top of the sand dune, and they couldn't believe what was in front of their eyes!

CHAPTER

The boys were gasping for air, and their mouths were so dry they could hardly speak. They didn't even dare open their mouths for fear they would dry up even more. As they stood there, folded at the waist, hands on their knees, Ryan lifted his arm and pointed straight ahead, then collapsed it back down to his knees, and took another giant breath in and out. Ryan finally regained his breath and said quietly, trying to conserve energy, "There it is. The object I saw from way back where we started."

Matthew acknowledged Ryan by nodding his head. He had no idea how Ryan had seen that from where they were originally standing. Maybe he didn't actually see anything. Maybe it was just a mirage he saw or some intuition that guided him, but it sure panned out to be something now. Something that was just within their reach.

"It looks like some kind of a stone ring on the desert ground," Matthew stated, with more of an expression of a question as it was hard to make out what exactly they were seeing.

Ryan nodded and continued to examine the object from afar, which was proving to be a diffcult task. It looked like an unusual type of stone. It had a reddish-orange tinge to it and looked like hardened sand. Suddenly he remembered what it was. It was sandstone.

Before Ryan could speak, Matthew suddenly declared, "Hey! That orange colored rock is sandstone. I remember that I read about it in my science book back in grade school. I remember it because you were sitting right next to me making weird faces at me and trying to make me laugh while I was trying to answer the teacher's question; we both ended up in detention!"

Matthew was so excited he had another memory of his childhood, even if it was a crazy one like this. Things were definitely starting to come back to him now as he remembered walking home from school with Ryan and playing in the yard together. In fact, he remembered them living right next door to each other! He felt himself drifting into several more memories, but he quickly tried to regain focus as he knew they were running out of time in the desert and needed to conquer the next challenge by quickly finding some water.

His energy perked up with these memories and he nudged Ryan on the shoulder as if he was waiting for congratulations. Ryan was simply too exhausted to oblige, but he gave him a thumbs up anyway. They started to make their way down from the peak of the sand dune to the base where the sandstone ring was resting on top of the desert sand.

As the boys got closer to the ring, a bad feeling overtook both of them and they instinctively knew something was about to happen. They approached the sandstone ring, and both boys knelt down to examine the rock. It looked like it was made of quartz-like grains, and the surface had a frosty appearance.

The boys were becoming familiar now with these circular obstacles they had encountered in both the jungle and the prairie, and as they traced their challenges back, they realized the next thing they needed to do was to get to the center of the ring in hopes there were food packets and water buried within the sand.

Before they stepped into the ring, the boys looked around and examined their surroundings. Everything looked perfectly fine. The wind had subsided, and the sand and dust had settled. The temperature continued to drop slightly. Although still very thirsty, the boys felt a slight sense of relief. Just the anticipation of potentially finding food and water was enough to keep them focused on what they needed to do next to get to the center of the ring. The boys assumed that everything would be fine, so they climbed over the rocks and stepped into the sandstone ring.

Within seconds, they heard a thundering roar from all around them. They turned around, backs against one another like they had done in the circular grove of trees on the prairie. From behind the sand dunes in the distance, they could see a herd of beasts coming toward them. The same type of beasts they had conquered twice before. Matthew reached into his backpack and grabbed the knife while Ryan looked around for something to defend himself.

Ryan started to run around the circle looking for anything he could use to fight off the beasts when suddenly he tripped. Something was sticking out of the ground. It was a bow and some arrows. Ryan remembered shooting a bow and arrow when he and his dad went on their hunting trips, and he knew exactly how to use them. These hidden supplies were a lifesaver. Ryan realized that sometimes things that are actually right there in front of us are unseen. If he hadn't looked, he wouldn't have found what he needed to hopefully conquer yet another challenge.

With weapons in hand, and the beasts gaining ground on them, the boys tried to find a way to shelter themselves behind the sandstone rocks. There was only one rock that was large enough to hide behind, and it wouldn't take much for the beasts to trample them once they reached the rocks. They needed to come together and develop a strategy that would work for both of them. Matthew only had a small knife, and there were only seven arrows that Ryan had counted after he dug the bow and arrows out of the sand.

Ryan quickly came up with a plan and without hesitation said to Matthew, "Let's let the beasts come to us. You swipe each beast's front legs with your knife and then go on to the next one. As they rear up, I will shoot the beasts in the chest with my bow and arrow. Depending on how many there are, we may need to try to salvage the arrows and reload."

"Got it!" Matthew said as he positioned himself close to the edge of the sandstone rocks.

He would be the first one to go after the beasts and he knew the risk he was taking. He closed his eyes and imagined himself encountering the beast. This was about to be the biggest challenge they had faced thus far on the island, and he knew he had to bring his warrior back. He had to overcome this obstacle, despite the fear he felt, despite the fatigue and dehydration, and despite the circumstance they were in. It was time to win this challenge. It was the only option.

Within seconds of finalizing their plan, the first beast rushed toward Matthew like a freight train coming down the track full throttle. When the beast got close enough to the sandstone rock, Matthew ran past it and cut its front legs with his knife. Green goo poured out from the flesh wounds, and the beast reared up onto its hind legs.

As the beast rose up, Ryan was standing on the opposite side of the stone ring and had loaded an arrow into his bow. He was about to take his first shot with a bow in what he believed to be a very long time. He trusted his instincts and pulled back his loaded bow and shot the first arrow straight toward the beast's chest.

As he took the shot, he knew he had hit the beast; he just didn't know where the arrow had landed. He could hear the beast roaring as he loaded the next arrow into his bow. He took a quick glance at the beast and saw he had hit it in the torso. He hoped the hit would be lethal, but he didn't know.

The beast roared as it sank down to the ground. It was severely wounded, but not dead yet. Before Ryan could get another shot off with his arrow, Matthew jumped in and stabbed it again, putting it out of its agony. As he did, the beast disappeared like the others had done, this time leaving behind food packets and water.

They boys were astonished, but they knew the battle had just begun. They could not be distracted by the shiny objects they had uncovered. Without celebrating the first victory, the boys prepared for the next group of beasts that was heading toward them. Their teamwork had once again proven to be the key to their success in killing the first beast, and they knew they would need to continue to work even closer together as the beasts were coming from all angles now, and they were indeed angry.

The beasts approached the sandstone within seconds, and there were too many to count this time. It would take everything the boys had left in them to fight this many off at a time. Matthew ran around the circle with the knife clenched tightly in his right hand and his arms flailing around, just trying to distract the beasts and hoping he would hit something as he ran around.

It was enough to anger the beasts even more and as they reared up, Ryan took a shot at the beast closest to him on the right. This time though, he missed. He started to panic. But, as he watched Matthew continuing to run around like a wild man, he knew he needed to keep it together or his friend would be the first one to suffer the wrath of the beasts. He was not about to let that happen.

Ryan reloaded his bow and shot an arrow again at the beast closest to him on the right. This time he actually hit it. The beast fell down and died. As he drew the next arrow into the bow, he saw one of the beasts suddenly change course and start charging toward Matthew. Ryan took aim and fired a shot directly in front of Matthew and in the area where the beast was headed.

As the beast continued to charge toward Matthew, it ran straight into the path of the flying arrow. The arrow sunk deep into the side of the beast. The beast collapsed and died. Had Ryan aimed where the beast was, it would have been too late. The arrow would have missed and Matthew would have been trampled and gone for sure! Matthew turned around almost in shock and stared at Ryan.

"Thanks, buddy!" Matthew quickly hollered as he regained his composure.

Matthew's acknowledgment had almost caused him to be trampled as the last round of beasts was coming faster than ever toward the boys. At the last second, he saw a beast coming directly toward him. He turned around and rolled to the side just in the nick of time.

Ryan loaded another arrow into the bow and shot the beast, this time hitting it in the leg. Matthew reached up from where he was lying and without hesitation stabbed it in the back. The beast let out its last roar and disappeared into the ground.

The boys continued to repeat this process until all of the beasts were gone. They fought valiantly to the end and, despite their fatigue and dehydration, they felt the energy of each victory surging through their veins as if it were a magic beverage filling them up from head to toe. As the last beast was defeated and dissipated into the hot desert sand, another round of food packets and water presented itself.

Although only the first and the last beast had the prize of the food packets and water, the boys were overjoyed they not only were alive and had survived the biggest challenge of their lives, but they finally had some fresh water and food.

CHAPTER

The boys collapsed onto the desert sand in the center of the sandstone ring and gathered up their prizes. They each chugged their first bottle of water down so quickly it almost made them sick. Both boys had finished their water in a matter of seconds. They opened their food packets and began to reflect on the challenge they had just faced.

Neither of the boys could understand why this was happening to them. They continued to debate who would be crazy enough to do this to someone. And, for what purpose? It was that question that triggered something in Matthew.

He had a few quick flashbacks of times when he had complained about what now seemed to be just little things in life. Small challenges that he had faced, but decided to turn away from and go in a different direction because he wasn't confident enough in himself. He remembered trying out for the basketball team. He was too slow and wasn't quite able to keep up with the other boys, so he just gave up. When he was put on the "B" team for baseball, he gave up trying to compete because he didn't think it mattered anyway.

Ryan also reflected on how he had always tried to do everything on his own. Sure, he had his best friend Matthew by his side, but he never really truly relied on the strength and support of his friend. He recalled the science fair project that went terribly wrong because he used the wrong template for his presentation, despite Matthew's attempts to help him correct it, so he failed the project. He always acted like he could handle everything on his own.

He then remembered some of the times before when he felt like he never had enough. Enough friends, enough toys, enough money, enough of anything. Like when his mom took him "back to school" shopping at the discount store, and he just knew all the other kids would come to school with the new trendy clothes and he would be stuck with the generic clothes. Or when they picked up his backpack and school supplies at the donation center because they couldn't afford to pay for both clothes and supplies.

Now the funny thing was, all he and Matthew had on this incredible journey was each other and a few minor necessities, and yet they were still alive. It was really all they needed. Was this the lesson they were supposed to receive? But who would be crazy enough to do this to them just to teach them a lesson?

The food packets and water were so refreshing. After devouring the nourishment, Matthew looked up at Ryan as he was licking his lips trying to get every last ounce of food he could and said, "Ryan, how did we make it this far without dying?"

Ryan responded without hesitation and assertively proclaimed, "Well, Matthew, it basically comes down to my pure skill, strength, and intellect."

"Yeah right! If that were the case, we wouldn't have even made it through the first night," Matthew exclaimed as he made one last attempt to get another drop of water out of his water bottle.

Ryan chucked his empty water bottle at Matthew and became more sincere, "Seriously though, I don't know how we made it this far, but I know that we couldn't have done it without each other. We've had too many close calls out here, but I think we've figured out this teamwork stuff by now."

Matthew agreed with Ryan and interjected, "Yeah, I bet whoever put us here didn't think we had it in us to get this far. What I can't believe is the fact that I'm definitely stronger now, we both are, and it seems like no matter what happens next, I'm just glad I've had my best friend with me in this game."

As the boys continued to reflect on the island games and their past, their memories were starting to come back stronger now, and they had finally reached the point of agreement that they were happier than they had ever been, even though none of this made any sense. They decided that although they might never know the "who" or the "why" behind all of this, they recognized the value of their friendship and the lessons they had learned along the way, throughout the journey they were on.

As they finished their last bites of their food packets and drank half of the last bottle of water to conserve the rest, they suddenly realized they had been talking so long that the sun was beginning to set and they had no idea where they were going to find shelter for the night.

They only knew they were too weak and exhausted to handle another round of the beasts, and they were sitting ducks on a pond for another round of beasts to come their way if they stayed out in the middle of the sandstone ring. The only problem was, there was nowhere for them to go.

They looked around and all they saw was a barren desert. It was the first time since they woke up on the shore of the mysterious island they would not have shelter or the warmth they would need to get through the night. This time, they would only have each other. After all they had gone through, they felt that was all they really needed to make it through another night on the mysterious island.

Ryan shivered. The air was starting to cool down rapidly now as the sun was beginning to set. Before they knew it, the lights would go out and it would be just them, under the desert stars, in the middle of the sandstone ring. They took their shirts off their heads and slipped them back on. Although they were disgustingly dirty and smelled rotten, the boys appreciated what they had and enjoyed the extra warmth. They grabbed their blankets out of their backpacks, wrapped themselves up, and huddled close together to prepare for a long night under the stars.

Just as the last sliver of sunlight danced across the desert sand and the moon took over the night sky, Matthew noticed a shiny reflection alongside one of the sandstone rocks. It was something he hadn't noticed before. He could tell Ryan was already starting to nod off, even though they were still sitting straight up, but he gave him a quick shove. Ryan jumped and opened his eyes. Matthew was right in front of Ryan's face. Ryan could literally feel the warmth of Matthew's breath on his face, and the smell of Matthew's rotten breath made him gag.

Matthew whispered, "Ryan, do you see that? That shiny

thing over there the moon is lighting up alongside that stone."

Ryan opened his eyes and said, "Dude, now you are really imagining things. Just close your eyes and let's tough this out. We will figure out what we are going to do in the morning."

Matthew was not about to let this one go. How could he possibly see something, or think he saw something, and not go after it? Hadn't they learned enough lessons along the way about taking risks and using their intuition? Well, this was for sure the time to do just that.

Matthew uncovered himself from his blanket and slowly crawled over to the area where he had seen the shiny object. In the dark of the night, Matthew reached out and grabbed the object. He brought it up toward his face to take a closer look. It was another key! This time, from what he could tell, it felt like a sandstone key.

Matthew quickly crawled back to Ryan and shook him to wake him from the sleep he had already dropped into. He flashed the key in front of Ryan's face. Ryan sat up, not really understanding what had gotten into his friend. That was, until he saw the key.

"Wow! Another stupid key," Ryan said sarcastically as he took the key from Matthew, looked at it, handed it back, and lay back down, rolling over to face in the opposite direction of Matthew.

"Seriously?" Matthew responded with a tone of voice that clearly told Ryan he was about to receive a lecture.

Ryan rolled his eyes and sat back up. This time, he gently took the key out of Matthew's hands and then grabbed Matthew's backpack to search for the other two keys. It was so dark, but the moon had started to glow in the sky and there was just enough light for Ryan and Matthew to compare the three keys they now had in their possession.

As the boys sat there, they turned the keys over and over in their hands, looking at each one as if they were examining them under a microscope. Although it was dark in the middle of the desert, they could see the similar etchings in the sides of all of the keys, and they all had the same teeth pattern. What could these possibly be for?

Matthew took the first two keys and gave the newest one to Ryan and said, "I don't know what they are for, but I think you should keep this one on you just in case something happens to me."

"All right. That was sappy and a little creepy. Now, can we just get some rest?" Ryan said sarcastically again, frustrated but trying not to offend his friend.

Ryan had had just about enough of this day and this long journey. The fatigue had definitely gotten the most of him. He just wanted to lie down and fall asleep and make it all go away. They had gone through enough already and had no idea what tomorrow would hold for them. It was time to call it quits for the day.

Matthew took his two keys and gently placed them into his backpack where he had originally pulled them from. He then wrapped himself back up in his blanket and lay down next to where Ryan was sitting. Ryan didn't have enough energy to try to apologize and comfort Matthew, and he certainly didn't have enough energy to put the key back into his backpack. Instead, he slammed the key into the sand next to him.

Just as the teeth of the key entered the sand, the ground began to quake. Matthew jolted up and threw the blanket aside. Both boys jumped to their feet, grabbed their backpacks, shoved their blankets inside, and were about to run. As Ryan reached to grab the key, it disappeared deep into the sand. At the same time, the boy's feet were sinking deep into the sand. They attempted to lift their feet, but couldn't. The ground had turned to quicksand. The sandstone ring had now become a quicksand death trap.

"What's happening?" Ryan screamed as he looked at Matthew and continued to try to pull his feet out of the ground.

"Dude! We are in quicksand. We are sinking!" Matthew hollered back as he attempted to pull his legs out by reaching down and grabbing his legs under his knees.

Nothing was working. They were sinking, and fast. As the quicksand continued to rise, the boys reached out toward the sandstone in an attempt to grab the stone, but they were too far away. There was nothing more they could do. They had fought every battle and had been victorious. They now knew this might be their last moment on the island and their last moment with each other.

It was a slow process that allowed them to hold on tight to each other and trust in the support they had in one another. As the quicksand continued to rise, it reached their chests and they could feel the pressure building inside their bodies. It felt as if they were being squeezed to death. That was, unfortunately, exactly what was happening.

There was nothing more the boys needed to reflect on. They had covered their journey together in their conversation earlier and they felt they had reconciled with all of their own beasts along the way. All they could do now was let the process take place as they had no more fight left in them. They had given everything they had.

With his last breath, Matthew looked at his best friend Ryan and said, "I love you, man!"

"Love you too! See you on the other side," Ryan quickly responded.

And then they were gone...

CHAPTER

Ryan gasped for air as he began to wake from the worst nightmare of his life! He wanted to sleep some more, but he was suddenly freezing. He rolled over and tried to pull the covers up over himself, but as he searched for the covers, he realized there weren't any there. Frustrated, he opened his eyes and his whole body began to shake uncontrollably.

He was not prepared for what he saw. He and Matthew had somehow ended up on the side of a mountain. Matthew was lying face down with his body sprawled out, legs and feet dangling just over the edge of the cliff. He could see Matthew's back rising with each breath he took, so Ryan knew Matthew was still alive. He just didn't know if he was conscious yet. Ryan realized his nightmare in his dreams was actually a living nightmare.

He knew he needed to wake Matthew up, but had to do so carefully; otherwise, Matthew would end up rolling off the side of the mountain. After everything they had gone through, Ryan was not about to let that happen. If they could survive being sucked under the earth in quicksand and practically squeezed to death, he knew they could survive anything.

Ryan carefully sat up and made his way into a crawling position on hands and knees. Before he moved, he assessed the edge of the cliff where they had landed and knew there was plenty of room behind him, just not so much around the edges. It was a narrow overhang and he would have to be careful about how he made his next move.

He slowly and steadily crept his way out toward the edge of the cliff and gently grabbed Matthew's arms, which were lying flaccid, straight out in front of him. Ryan started to pull Matthew toward him while still trying to keep his balance in a crawling position. As he made the second pull, Matthew's head shot up and he pulled his arms back as if to protect himself from what he must have thought was another attack. "Ahhhh! What's going on?" Matthew screamed as he tried to escape the clutches of Ryan's hands.

Ryan quickly cut him off from the series of questions he anticipated were about to flow from Matthew's mouth and said in as calm and soothing voice as he possibly could, "Matthew, it's me, Ryan. You need to calm down and listen to me. You are in a dangerous spot right now and you need to let me pull you back toward me…"

Before Ryan could finish by saying, "and whatever you do, don't look down," Matthew pulled his arms back away from the grip Ryan had on them and turned his head to look around. He immediately froze and dug his fingers into the rocky ground of the cliff. Ryan remained in the same position he was in and carefully reached back out to Matthew, motioning for him to do the same so he could grab his arms.

This time, Matthew complied as he trembled from head to toe. Ryan pulled and slid backward, pulled and slid backward, and then on the third pull, Matthew's feet were safely back on the cliff. He crawled the rest of the way toward the side of the mountain where Ryan was now sitting. Both boys rested their backs against the side of the mountain and curled up into as tight a ball as they could to keep warm. They blew into their hands to warm them up and took a few moments to assess their current situation before they spoke. Ryan was, of course, the first to chime in and said, "Well, I guess I did ask for a cooler climate."

Matthew looked at him and smiled. He was not surprised by his friend's crazy comment. In fact, by now, he kind of expected it. He was still confused as to what had just happened, as the last thing he remembered was telling Ryan he loved him. Now he was starting to feel a bit weird about having said that since they were still alive and all. He was hoping Ryan might just forget about that last comment he made before they got sucked under the earth.

"What happened? How in the world do you suppose we got here? The last thing I remember was being sucked under the earth by the quicksand and now we are here? And where is here, anyway?" Matthew said with a series of loaded questions and pressured speech, hoping Ryan could clear some of this up for him.

Ryan looked at Matthew and rolled his eyes and jokingly said, "Really? 'Cause the last thing I remember was you telling me you loved me."

Matthew's hope for Ryan's short-term memory loss had obviously not occurred during the transport from the desert to the side of the mountain. Although Ryan had said the same thing back to Matthew, he knew Ryan wouldn't let this one go unless he quickly changed the subject.

Matthew knew he needed to refocus to figure out where they were going to move to next. He realized it wouldn't take long for them to freeze in the elements they were now facing. Moving forward had consistently been one of their keys to survival along this journey, and they didn't want to waste any time doing just that.

The boys pulled their backpacks toward them, slowly got to their feet, and carefully slipped their backpacks on backward onto the front of their chests. They stood with their backs pressed against the side of the mountain, while still clinging onto the mountain with their arms outstretched and fingers digging into the rocky terrain.

They were both a little dizzy when they stood, and they took another moment to get their bearings. They were still weak and extremely tired since, as far as they could tell, they didn't actually get any sleep aside from the time they had been passed out on the cliff. It was hardly what they could quantify as quality sleep in those conditions.

Matthew motioned for Ryan to follow him as he had spotted a path that ran alongside the mountain on the side he was standing. Without hesitation, Ryan followed and they made their way across the rugged path to an area that opened up in front of them. Once they had reached what they considered to be solid ground, they switched their backpacks around to their backs and took a moment to look around.

As they scanned the area around them, they could see the

large volcano looming again in the distance above the thick collection of pine trees and the rugged mountain peaks. Although they had seen the volcano from the jungle, prairie, and the desert, it appeared now to be closer than it had ever been. They again recognized that although they were obviously in a different climate in a different quadrant of the island, they had to be on the same island, as the volcano had been their consistent landmark throughout the journey they were on.

They were relieved to be off the cliff, but they knew their time to strategize would be limited as the temperature was continuing to drop and they were already freezing. Matthew spotted something ahead of them and motioned for Ryan to follow again. They continued to move through the rocky terrain and under the towering pine trees. As they were moving in the direction of whatever it was Matthew had spotted in the distance, small white flakes started floating down from the sky.

Both boys wondered what it was. They figured it must be snow, but since the lighter fluid event, they were not about to take any chances. Nothing had ever been a for sure thing on the island. Ryan stuck his hand out and let a flake fall onto his palm. He then took his pointer finger from his other hand and dabbed it. It melted quickly and he proceeded to lick his finger. Matthew watched the whole thing unfold as if it was a slow motion video and couldn't help but remember the time he had to watch Ryan dig in his ears and pick his nose in the desert. It was enough of a memory to quickly prompt Matthew to get Ryan to stop.

"All right already! Just tell me what it is. I can't stand to watch you any longer," Matthew said with disgust in his voice.

Ryan stuck his tongue out and let the white flakes fall onto it and responded, "My scientific testing has determined that it's indeed snow."

"Well, what do you know. It looks like a duck, quacks like a duck, it is a duck," Matthew said, trying to remember where he had learned that saying from.

"Quack, quack. We need to get moving or we are going to be dead ducks," Ryan said as he could tell the temperature was continuing to drop and the snowfall was starting to intensify.

Matthew nodded in agreement as he noticed his shirt and pants were now covered in snow and really wet. The wet snow made everything on his body feel even colder than it was, and he knew if they didn't find shelter soon, they would both end up with frostbite. He recognized the signs of frostbite, and he could tell it was already setting in on the tips of his cold fingers. His toes and feet would soon be next.

"We have to find shelter fast or we are going to get frostbite," Ryan said as the snow thickened.

"We are getting closer. It's just over there," Matthew said as he picked up his pace.

The snow was coming down even harder now and the wind was starting to pick up. It was so thick, they almost couldn't see each other. Matthew grabbed onto Ryan and held on to him so they wouldn't get separated in the thick snow. It was painful to bend his fingers, but he knew it would be even worse if they lost each other in the storm.

As the boys pushed on, they began to lose the feeling in their arms and legs. They knew this was a bad sign, and now they really needed to get to the shelter Matthew had spotted, or else they would die. Suddenly, Ryan stumbled and collapsed on the ground. As he lay there, he felt the comfort of the ground and just wanted to sleep. For some reason, the ground felt warm and inviting.

Matthew pulled him back up and forced him to keep moving. Matthew knew Ryan was experiencing hypothermia, but if they stopped, they would die. Ryan grudgingly stood up with Matthew's help and continued to move his body forward. Although he could no longer feel his body, he instinctively kept the motion of his legs and arms in sync with Matthew. It took everything he had to continue to press on.

As the boys passed a group of tightly intertwined pine trees, they saw what Matthew had spotted in the distance. Rising up in the sky was a giant ice cave! It was the most beautiful shelter they had ever seen. There were giant ice crystals dangling down from the sides of the mountain. It had created a large cave the boys were able to crawl into and escape from the pounding wind and snow.

As they crawled into the ice cave, they could feel the wind ease off their skin and the snow starting to melt off their clothes. Although the shelter was a blessing, they needed to rewarm themselves quickly. Ryan had already collapsed onto a rock inside the cave and was shaking from head to toe. Matthew looked around inside the cave to see if there was anything he could find to cover his friend up. Even pine branches would be better than nothing at this point, but he knew he couldn't go back outside and risk getting lost in the snowfall that had now become a full-fledged blizzard. There had to be something he could find inside the cave and once he did, he needed to find a way to quickly build a fire.

Matthew rubbed Ryan's arms briskly, covered him with the blanket he pulled out of the backpack, and said, "I'm going to explore some more caverns within the cave to see if I can find anything to warm us up. Hang on, buddy."

Matthew's feet and legs were so cold they felt like the tree stumps they had sat on so many times in the jungle. As he wandered through the dimly lit ice cave that had been created off the side of the mountain, he found himself longing to be back in the jungle. He remembered it being so beautiful, and aside from the beasts and the wicked temple, he felt like they could have at least found a way to survive in that environment.

Not here, though, in what appeared to be highlands. Not in these conditions. Nothing could survive, and neither would they unless they found something to warm them up. As he continued to search the ice cave, he recalled the four different areas they had now been in on the island – the jungle, prairie, desert, and now, the highlands. He hoped this would be the last of the quadrants, and after they conquered this challenge, they would win the island games and be released from the island to go back to wherever it was they came from.

His mind continued to drift back to the challenges they had faced along the way. It was enough to keep his energy up. He crawled through what appeared to be the last cavern within the ice cave, and that was when he found exactly what he had been envisioning and praying for all along their hike to the giant ice cave!

CHAPTER  19

Matthew had discovered a large pile of fur! It was almost like what he envisioned in his mind had become a reality. Either way, he didn't care how it happened. He was just thankful he found something that would provide some temporary relief from the cold and help to warm them both. Once they warmed up, he could go back outside and gather some wood to start a fire. He had to gather up the fur and get it back to Ryan quickly before Ryan's body temperature dropped even more than it already had.

As Matthew approached the pile of fur, he bent down to scoop it up and discovered there were actually two fur blankets and two fur coats along with food packets and water. He shook his head and realized that these must be the prizes for them being able to survive the challenge they had just faced. Although he was so relieved and grateful, he instantly became extremely angry again at whoever was doing this to them. Why them? Why this place? Hadn't they already gone through enough and learned enough lessons?

He knew he didn't have time to dwell on this as he needed to get the blankets and coats back to Ryan. He put one of the fur coats on, and as he made his way back through the caverns toward the open cave where he had left Ryan, he thought again about the game they were being forced to play. As he reflected, he felt bad for feeling angry and realized that it's not really about what life throws your way, because bad things can happen and, oftentimes, to really good people. It's really about how you face those challenges. As he thought about this, he wondered silently if he and Ryan really had what it would take to win this game.

Before long, he made his way back to the opening of the cave and found Ryan where he had left him. He was drifting in and out of consciousness and was calling out for his "mommy" again, just as he had when they were in the jungle. *This was a good sign,* Matthew thought to himself as he proceeded to cover Ryan up. As long as he didn't think Matthew was his mommy, they would be in good shape. Matthew rolled Ryan up like a hotdog in a bun and then proceeded to wrap himself up in the warm fur blanket. He wanted to dive into the food packets and water, but he felt it would be unfair to Ryan so he just settled in and leaned his back against a rock. And then he waited.

He waited for the feeling to come back into his fingers and toes. He waited for the warmth of the blanket to surge through the rest of his body. He waited for Ryan's breathing to slow down, back to a normal rate. He waited for the wind to stop howling and the snow to subside. He just sat there and waited.

As Matthew waited, he slipped into a light sleep...*Matthew was back in his home with his mom and dad. They were all watching a movie, like he remembered they did most Friday nights. The fireplace was dancing with the warm flames and the smell of popcorn was in the air. They were all laughing and happy to have the time together. He wanted to stay, but he knew he needed to leave for some reason. He felt like he was being pulled from the place he was at and eventually he woke from his sleep.*

He wasn't sure how long he had been sleeping, but he woke up with a sudden sense of anxiety that crept into his once peaceful state of sleep. He could tell the sun had now set, and the only light that remained in the ice cave was from the reflection of the moonlight dancing off the ice crystals hanging down over the entrance of the cave.

He was finally warmer, but needed to figure out a way to get a fire started. He also knew he needed to wake Ryan and get some food into both of their weak bodies. As he shuffled his hands around to search for his backpack, he heard Ryan let out a light moan.

Matthew crawled over to Ryan and gently said, "Hey, buddy. Did you enjoy your nap while I busted my butt and did all the work around here?"

"Wow, I was until I woke up and saw your ugly face," Ryan responded weakly with as much sarcasm as he could muster up.

"Atta boy! Welcome back, my friend," Matthew said with a sense of relief.

Ryan rolled himself over and propped himself back up against the rock he had been leaning on when they first entered the cave. He had no idea what he was wrapped up in, but it sure felt good. He was grateful to have feeling in all of his body parts once again. He remembered how awful he felt when they first got to the cave, and then from there, he couldn't remember anything.

Matthew interrupted Ryan's thoughts and continued on to say, "Now that you are alive again, we need to figure out how to get a fire going. If we can find something in here to get a small fire started, it will provide us enough light and warmth and then I can go outside and try to find some branches to keep it going. Oh, and before I forget, I have another surprise for you if you are a really good boy while I'm gone."

"Seriously! You are going to make me puke if you keep that up," Ryan said with very little patience as he started to dig around in his backpack looking for the matches and possibly something to use to get the fire started.

Matthew grinned from ear to ear. *It was so good to have his best friend back on planet earth, if that was indeed where they were,* he thought to himself as he began to prepare to go back out into the snowy mountain range. Matthew couldn't wait to share the surprise with Ryan, so he chucked a food packet and some water at Ryan's feet and Ryan flashed a big grin. Although they were both hungry and thirsty, they knew they needed to get the fire going before they indulged in another "gourmet" meal.

Ryan took his hands out of the blanket he had been tucked into the last several hours and started digging in the snow to create a small fire pit. He then opened up his backpack to see if there was anything he would be willing to part with to burn until they could get some wood from outside. As he dug through his backpack, he felt the sandstone key Matthew had discovered within the sandstone ring in the desert.

Somehow, although the key had disappeared in the quicksand, it made it back into his backpack and was now safely tucked away. *Another mystery of the island games,* he thought to himself as he continued to evaluate his options for something to burn. All he could find in his backpack to burn was the rope. He wasn't sure if he could get it started, or if he could even keep it burning, but there was literally nothing else he could think of to burn.

Ryan knew the risk was huge. If they had not had the rope when he had fallen into the pit in the prairie, there would have been no way he would have made it out. And, it was the rope that allowed them to get the food packets, water, and key off the rising platform in the prairie. Just as the rope had saved them in the prairie, it would be needed to save them again in the ice cave. Right now, it was their only chance to get the fire started.

"It's a shame we have to burn this, but it's the only thing I could find to burn. I sure hope we don't regret this," Ryan said as he wound the rope up into as tight a circular mound as he could, lit a match, and then started the rope on fire.

As the rope began to burn, the boys could instantly feel the additional layer of cold melting off them. They crowded around the smoldering fire and put their hands up close to it. Both boys had a tingling feeling in their hands as the rope provided just enough warmth to fight the cold, damp air they were exposed to in the cave. For a moment, they just sat there and talked about how thankful they were they had found the ice cave.

Matthew got up from the fire and adjusted the fur blanket so it was draped around his lower body to protect the bottom of his exposed legs. He walked over to the entrance of the cave and crouched down to look out the mouth of the cave. He could tell the blizzard had died down, but it was still snowing and now even more diffcult to see since it was dark outside. The dense pine trees served as a bit of a barricade from the wind and snow, but made it harder to see as the thick covering blocked the light from the moon.

If Matthew was to be successful in retrieving some branches, he would have to find them close enough to the cave to avoid being out in the harsh elements for too long. And, more importantly, he needed to be able to find his way back to the cave. He knew he didn't have a choice but to go out and find some branches; it was time for him to begin his search. He also knew it would not be safe for Ryan to attempt to help him, so he needed to get moving on his own. He dropped the fur blanket on the frozen ground of the cave and made his way out into the dark night.

Ryan looked over at the entrance to the cave and just as he did, Matthew disappeared into the snowy night. He could hear Matthew shuffling through the trees and would occasionally hear him grunt as he tossed something toward the cave entrance. Ryan brought himself to a stand and gave himself time to adjust to the head rush he experienced. He was definitely the weakest he had been since they arrived on the island.

After a moment, he put the other fur coat on that Matthew had retrieved for him and then adjusted his blanket around his lower body as Matthew had, and walked over to the entrance of the cave. As he looked out in hopes of seeing Matthew, he started thinking about how they had transitioned from climate to climate and yet, they must still be on the same island they had originally washed up on. Right?

He couldn't help but wonder if the whole island was actually some kind of indoor bubble and the gamekeepers were just adjusting the temperature to be too hot or too cold just to tick them off. If they were inside some kind of a bubble, then maybe they actually needed to be looking for a way up instead of a way off the island. Maybe they had to find a way to climb up before they could get out.

Ryan thought he might be onto something now, and he could feel the adrenaline start to build again. But, he still couldn't help but wonder how the gamekeepers could possibly be making all of this happen. They had to have some kind of wind machine to have caused the sand to blow in their faces in the desert and the snow to whip them insultingly in the frozen highlands. The island games were really starting to tick him off now. Now all he wanted to do was conquer it to prove that he and Matthew were really stronger than the gamekeepers must have thought they were.

Ryan broke himself out of his own trance and stepped outside the cave and found the pile of branches Matthew had been tossing toward the entrance. He called out to Matthew and Matthew acknowledged that he was okay, so Ryan grabbed a bundle of pine branches and tossed them into the cave.

They had quite the assembly line going for a while, with Matthew sourcing the branches and Ryan piling them up inside the cave. He stoked the fire and by the time Matthew got back inside, the cave was starting to heat up nicely. The crystals of ice reflected the flames from the fire and the entire cave was soon sparkling. The boys settled in next to the fire with their coats on and the blankets of fur wrapped tightly around them. They finally opened the food packets and discovered the flavor of the night was steak.

While they enjoyed their food and drank their water, Matthew shared with Ryan how he had found the pile of fur coats and blankets along with the food packets and water. Ryan then shared with Matthew how he thought they might be in some kind of climate-controlled bubble and they needed to find a way up before they could find a way out.

Ryan explained as Matthew listened intently, "I think this island, if that is what we are really on, is inside some kind of climate-controlled bubble. The gamekeepers are obviously having a good time playing with the temperature control, but I'm thinking in order to win this game, we need to find a way up before we can find a way out."

"Yeah, you might be onto something, Ryan. My vote is this place is indoors and there is an invisible bubble around us. It may even have something to do with the invisible wall we ran into in the jungle. Maybe if we found a way to that volcano, there will be a way to get up and out just as you have described," Matthew said as he was starting to get excited about the potential to win the game and get off the mysterious island.

The boys continued to talk and strategize about potential ways to beat the island games, and as they did, they both gradually became more and more drowsy. Despite the fatigue, they continued to discuss the three quadrants of the island they had already conquered and wondered what other challenges would lie ahead in the fourth quadrant they were now in.

As their conversation began to die down and they were now feeling more content with some food in their bellies, they started to refill their empty water bottles with some snow from around the floor of the cave so it could melt and allow them more water in the morning. They packed the empty water bottles with snow and then settled back in around the fire.

They decided to get really comfortable and dug out two areas near the fire making a body-shaped hole for them to lay their blankets in and curl up. They were bound and determined to get a good night's sleep and stay as warm as possible. They climbed into their little cocoons and lay down next to the smoldering fire. As they did, they immediately felt their bodies relax, and they drifted peacefully off to sleep...

Suddenly, there was a loud cracking sound that came from the depths of the ice cave! The boys both jumped up, having become familiar with these unexpected sounds. They looked around but saw nothing. The fire was still burning, and they figured it must have just been the fire and the heat causing some shifting of the ice cave. Before long, the boys had curled back up and drifted off.

As Matthew and Ryan drifted off, they both fell deep into a dream-like state. Matthew could feel himself being pulled back into a place that felt so familiar, yet frightening. He tried to resist, but despite his efforts, he lost the battle. *There was a loud popping sound and suddenly, Matthew awoke in the same white room he and Ryan had been in before. As he looked around the room, he saw Ryan sleeping in the other bed in the center of the room. There were no other sounds other than that of Ryan's restless breathing, so Matthew knew Ryan was alive and he felt a slight sense of relief.*

As Matthew quietly slipped off the bed onto the cold sterile floor, the same feeling of confusion came back over him. Were they dreaming? Had they been rescued? Or, was this a trap? Why were they in the same place again? Matthew attempted to wake Ryan, but it was no use, he just couldn't wake him from his deep sleep. Instead of waiting for Ryan to wake up, Matthew knew he had to do something, so he took his first few steps toward the door with the reflective glass window.

He approached the door slowly as he remembered last time, or at least in his last vision that was exactly like this, he and Ryan were overtaken by the green gas that knocked them out. This time, he wanted to do anything he could to get outside that door and try to get help. Matthew made it to the door and this time, no green gas overtook him. For now, he was safe. He reached out to grab the door handle and closed his eyes, as he was afraid of what was next.

This time, the door was unlocked! He took a quick peek back at Ryan, who was still in a deep sleep and knew that he had to leave his buddy behind this time if they were going to make it out of this place alive. Matthew pulled the door handle down toward the floor, and the door made a soft click and opened without any resistance. He carefully stuck his head out the door and looked both ways down the long corridor, and after seeing nobody in the hallway, he began to move quietly down the sterile corridor.

Matthew didn't know quite what he was looking for, but he had it in his mind to find some kind of way to signal for help, like a phone or a computer or something, anything at this point. As he made his way down the hall, he looked into each room, both on his right and on his left, and all he saw was the same two beds in the center of each white room.

However, as he reached the end of the hallway, there was a circular room that looked like a huge control center filled with computers and other equipment that he had never seen before. He quickly snuck into the room and tried to find a computer that was on so he could attempt to signal for help. As he made his way through the aisles of computers, he suddenly heard the soft sound of footsteps drawing near. Matthew quickly ducked and hid under the desk as he trembled with fear.

He then heard the sound of whispering and finally made out what the voice was saying, "Matthew, I know you're in here. Come out. It's me..."

Matthew was jolted awake again by a loud popping sound. He quickly looked around and realized that he was back in the ice cave, with Ryan right next to him by the fire. Matthew was confused once again by this strange vision, and he wanted to talk to Ryan about it, but he was so exhausted and Ryan was so restless that he didn't want to wake him because of another silly dream. Matthew figured he would just talk to Ryan about this dream tomorrow. If he wasn't so tired, he would get up and look to see what that popping sound was, but, he just couldn't bear the thought of getting out of his nice warm blanket. With that last thought, he was fast asleep.

CHAPTER 20

After a long, restless night of sleep, the boys awoke to yet another unfamiliar sound. It was a loud moaning noise combined with intermittent cracking and popping noises, similar to what they heard just as they were falling asleep. Both boys sat up immediately, wondering what the noise was. Matthew remembered the crazy dream and the popping sound he heard but had ignored because he had been too exhausted to care.

Just then, the boys heard the familiar noise of Reggie's cock-a-doodle-doo. This time, they couldn't have cared less since they were already awake and were more concerned about the noises they were hearing inside the cave. Matthew regretted not telling Ryan about it now because he realized there was something really wrong. It almost sounded like the ice cave was about to collapse.

Matthew looked at Ryan and then looked up and saw a large crack directly above them and said, "I forgot to tell you about this noise I heard last night. It was like a loud popping noise. I heard it after the cracking noise we both heard and then was just too tired to care. I thought it might just be the fire."

The crack ran the whole length of the cave and was about a

foot wide. The boys were now hustling to gather up their supplies, including the extra water they had melted from the snow they had loaded into their bottles the night before. They quickly took the fur coats and secured them tightly in place around their bodies, but made the decision to leave the fur blankets as they would not fit in their backpacks. They kept the small blankets and packed the rest of their supplies as fast as they could.

They were both frustrated with themselves for not doing this last night when they should have. They had talked about what they would need for warmth when they went back outside in the morning to continue their journey, but they were simply too tired at that point to do anything about it. The warm fur blankets were even toastier next to the fire, and they simply didn't want to climb out at that point last night.

As they hustled around the cave getting ready to exit, Ryan was obviously frustrated with Matthew and finally said, "Why didn't you tell me about that noise last night? We could have moved or at least done something, like prepare to move. Now the cave might collapse on us and we will both be dead."

At first Matthew simply ignored the glare and comment he received from Ryan. They both knew there was a blizzard still whipping through the highlands last night and neither one of them was in any shape to go anywhere. However, he knew Ryan was right. He should have woken Ryan up to at least tell him what he heard.

They had survived because of teamwork and trust, and Matthew started to feel a bit shameful that he had selfishly ignored the signs of danger to stay snuggled up in the comfy cocoon. He would be careful not to make the same mistake again. His only hope was that it was not too late now.

Matthew stopped what he was doing and said with sincerity, "I'm really sorry, Ryan, for letting you down and putting us in danger. I won't let that happen again."

Another loud crack and pop rang through the ice cave, and the boys looked up and saw the crack had widened significantly. Suddenly, a huge ice chunk fell down from the ceiling and landed directly behind them. Had they been standing a few steps further back, the boys would have been crushed! Before long, the entire ceiling of the cave began to collapse around them.

The boys dove toward the mouth of the cave, and as they did, Matthew stumbled and fell. Ryan looked back and then crawled over to Matthew while dodging falling ice chunks. He grabbed Matthew's hand and pulled Matthew toward him. They both dove out the mouth of the ice cave at the last second, just before the entire cave collapsed!

Once the boys had escaped the mouth of the ice cave, they bolted toward the safety of the thick pine forest to shield themselves from the aftermath of the crumbling cave. When they felt they were far enough away, they sat down for a moment under the trees to catch their breath. The air was still crisp, but the temperature was warmer than it had been when they arrived the day before.

The snow had subsided and there were no signs of the cruel conditions they had previously faced. The snow-covered ground glistened in the sun and was the only remnant of the blizzard that had nearly taken their lives the day before. At the same time, without speaking a word, Matthew and Ryan each gathered up a wad of snow, shaped them into the tightest snowballs they could, and flung the snowballs at each other.

They ran around the pine forest and dodged between the trees to protect themselves while escaping the snowballs hurtling toward them. For a period of time they had forgotten where they were, the island games they were playing, and instead embraced the wonder of the highlands and the snowball fight they were having with each other. It became the ultimate game of survival as the speed and intensity with which the boys were throwing snowballs at each other soon turned into a war.

The boys ran around the pine forest for what seemed like hours and before long, they found themselves in a different location. They looked back and couldn't even see the remnants of the ice cave they had found shelter in the night before. Where were they now? They had definitely lost track of the direction they were moving in and were genuinely lost in their snow war.

As they looked around to orientate themselves to their new surroundings, they located a river running in the valley of the mountain they hadn't seen before. Either they hadn't seen it because the blizzard was so thick or because they were miles away from where they had arrived on the mountain. Either way, they determined they would work their way down the sloping rocky terrain of the mountain and head toward the river.

As they arrived at the riverbank, they could see the rushing current making its way around the large rocks sticking up just above the water. Beyond the series of rocks within the river, there was an object they couldn't quite make out from where they were standing. Ryan ran over to the base of the mountain they had just crawled down and found a sturdy tree to climb. He dangled out onto the limb like he had done in the jungle when they were about to attack his "girlfriend," and he could now see what the object was.

"It's another circular platform, Matthew!" Ryan hollered from atop the tree limb.

Matthew looked back at Ryan swinging down from the limb like a monkey and said, "Seriously? Not another one. I'm not ready for this again and besides, how in the heck are we going to make it out to that platform? Can't you see how strong the current is rushing against those rocks? Even worse, I can't imagine how freezing cold the water is right now. No way! Uh-uh! I'm not going!"

Ryan finally jumped down off the tree limb and ran back over to where Matthew was throwing his temper tantrum and said, "Wow! That was intense. Are you done now?"

Matthew went over to the riverbank, picked up a dead branch sticking out of the snow, and promptly stuck it into the river. It immediately froze and turned into ice. Their eyes widened as they looked at each other with a renewed sense of fear. Neither one of them was prepared to die from drowning in the freezing water; this certainly did not appear to be an ordinary cold river.

"Wow! That is really cold if the branch froze the second we put it into the river. If we fall in, then we are dead for sure," Matthew said as he continued to shake his head to indicate he didn't want any part of the next challenge.

"So, let's just make sure we don't fall in," Ryan said calmly as he bent over to examine the stick.

Matthew continued on his rant and said, "What good will it do us to risk our lives to reach that platform anyway? We have no idea what is even on it, and based on the other games we have played on this creepy island, it will likely result in nothing but another nightmare."

Ryan hadn't seen Matthew react this way before, and he knew he needed to reassure him because he had seen what was on the platform. He just hadn't had the chance to tell Matthew what he saw because of the tantrum he was throwing.

Ryan walked back over to Matthew, grabbed his shoulders, and shook him a bit, hoping to shake some sense back into him, and said, "But I did see what was on the platform. I could see it from the tree. There are food packets, water, and I think there is another key! It was hard to tell, but I'm pretty sure it was another key. It could very well be what we need to get out of here. I know it is dangerous, but I don't see any other alternative. The gamekeepers have obviously set the bait, and now we need to fish."

Matthew hadn't realized that Ryan had actually seen what was on the platform, and he suddenly started to feel stupid about his childish temper tantrum. What had happened to the warrior he had pulled out so many times? Why hadn't he just stayed in that state so he could have been prepared for anything that came their way instead of whining like a little baby?

He then recognized that if he did stay in his warrior state all the time, he probably wouldn't survive very long because the feelings he had during those moments of fight were so intense. It just wouldn't be reasonable to live that way. In fact, it was almost exhausting, and he knew it wasn't sustainable.

He determined he just needed to be more aware of himself and remain calm in the eye of the storm, kind of like a wizard.

Wizards need to be calm and collected, even under the worst circumstances. Then when he needed to fight, he could pull the warrior out. He suddenly felt brilliant. Like the weight of the world had been lifted off his shoulders, and he was now ready to pull the warrior sword out and fight again.

As Matthew refocused his thoughts back to the group of rocks he was examining, he realized the way the rocks were grouped, they almost looked like a bridge to the platform. He finally said to Ryan, "I think what we are going to have to do is jump from rock to rock until we can make it to that big rock closest to the platform. From there, we are going to have to jump as hard as we can to land on the platform. It looks like it might be just as far as when you made that jump from the jungle platform."

"Well, it's about time you snapped out of it. I knew you would. Now, let's stop planning and talking and get going," Ryan said as he started off toward the riverbank.

Ryan made the jump to the first rock and looked back at Matthew with a huge grin of accomplishment. As he jumped to the second rock, he slipped a bit but managed to hold on. Once he steadied himself, he motioned for Matthew to follow. Matthew followed behind by jumping to the first rock and nearly slipped off right away, but regained his balance at the last second.

The adrenaline kicked in and the boys were now leaping from rock to rock while remaining focused on their goal of the platform. They were now too far into the river to turn back. They needed to remain steadfast on their goal and the prize ahead. They had faced these challenges before and reminded themselves that they could win this game too. As they got closer to the middle set of rocks along the way to the platform, they saw something suddenly flash by within the river water that was flowing aggressively under them.

"What the heck was that?" Ryan yelled as he pointed to where he saw the huge black streak.

Ryan had nearly thrown himself off balance from his sudden reaction. He looked around again quickly with sheer panic, trying to see where the streak had disappeared to. Ryan thought it looked almost like a huge black shark. Just then, from the corner of his eye, he saw something jump out of the water. He shifted his weight back and turned his head just in time to come face to face with a giant water beast! The water beast's mouth full of sharp teeth was wide open and poised to swallow him!

CHAPTER 21

At the last second, Ryan ducked out of the way, and the water beast splashed back into the water. Ryan was freaked out and quickly jumped to the next rock. He had a flashback to when the shark attacked him while he and Matthew were swimming toward the cargo boat. The fear of losing his pants again or being eaten alive was enough to kick-start the adrenaline rush. Before long, he had jumped several rocks and was now closer to the platform. He turned around and saw that Matthew was still safe, but moving a lot faster now too.

"Keep going!" Matthew yelled as he motioned frantically for Ryan to turn around and keep moving in the direction of the platform.

As Ryan turned back toward the platform, Matthew saw the water beast circle around to take another shot at swallowing Ryan. Just as it jumped in the air, Ryan leaped forward and landed in the middle of the platform, barely dodging the sharp teeth of the water beast. As Ryan rolled onto the platform, escaping the clutches of the water beast's mouth, he quickly got to his feet and motioned for Matthew to jump.

Matthew sailed through the air and jumped onto the platform but landed with only the upper half of his body on the platform and the lower half of his body dangling like fresh bait in the free air. It was as if he was taunting the water beast by flashing lunch right in front of its ugly face. Ryan dropped down to his belly, slid closer to the edge of the platform, and grabbed Matthew's wrists. He pulled Matthew quickly to the safety of the platform.

Matthew sat up and then helped Ryan up. Still out of breath, Matthew nodded at his friend to acknowledge him for saving his life again. It had been back and forth along this journey with each of them coming to the rescue of the other when they each were faced with such intense danger. They knew if they could survive and somehow find their way out, the impact of these experiences in the island games would change their lives forever.

Ryan was still out of breath, but crawled over to where the food packets, water, and key were lying near the edge of the platform. Ryan must have accidentally kicked the prizes toward the edge when he was trying to rescue Matthew. He couldn't help but think that it was a good thing he hadn't kicked them right off the edge into the frigid water. Ryan made his way back to where Matthew was still sitting with his arms wrapped around his knees and head resting on them.

Ryan dangled the prizes in front of Matthew and exclaimed, "Matthew! Let's take the food, water, and key and get the heck out of here."

There was no time to stop to eat or drink, or even examine the new key they had acquired, as their time was indeed bound to be short on the platform. Unexpectedly, the water beast jumped up directly behind Matthew with another attempt at lunch! Ryan shoved Matthew out of the way just in the nick of time. A few more seconds and Matthew would have been in the belly of the relentless water beast.

"Thanks, dude. I didn't see that ugly thing coming," Matthew said as he adjusted his fur coat to take his backpack off and pull out his knife.

Matthew had a plan to stab the beast when it jumped at them again, and this was his first opportunity to grab the knife from his backpack. He moved quickly and put his backpack on, brought the fur coat up over his shoulders, and tightened it securely around his body. Just then, he saw the water beast circle around behind Ryan and lunge forward near Ryan's head.

This time, Matthew shoved Ryan out of the way and stabbed the water beast right between the eyes. The upper half of the water beast's body flopped onto the platform and died. The boys were grossed out, but proceeded to inspect it anyway and determined that the water beast looked like a mix of a piranha and a crocodile. It had the body of the crocodile with the fins of a fish, was black from head to tail, and had hundreds of teeth like those of a piranha.

"Dude! That thing is so ugly it makes me want to barf just looking at it," Ryan said as he stared at the beast.

Just as Ryan finished making his horrid gagging motion, the water beast's body melted away. Ryan was relieved he didn't have to look at that ugly thing anymore. When the beast finally disappeared, Ryan shuddered and remembered the close moment when the beast had almost eaten him. How disgusting it would have been to be in the belly of that thing!

Ryan still had the prizes clutched tightly in his arms, so Matthew reached over and grabbed half of the food packets and water and was about to tuck them into his backpack when he realized he must have knocked the key out of Ryan's hand. The key was now dangling on the edge of the platform. Matthew dove for the key and grabbed onto it at the last possible second. But as he did, the platform shifted and Matthew started sliding off.

Ryan immediately felt the shifting of the platform. He dropped down to his belly again and dove to grab onto Matthew's feet. Luckily, Ryan's feet had anchored him by hooking onto the edge of the platform, and he managed not to slide off. Ryan pulled Matthew back into the center of the platform, and the shifting of their weight back to the center caused the platform to stabilize. Ryan took the key and put it carefully into his backpack and then situated his fur coat back onto his shoulders.

It certainly hadn't been easy to maneuver through the rock obstacle course with the big fur coats on and their backpacks weighing them down. They looked like camels crossing the river, but they knew the fur coats were saving them from another round of hypothermia and frostbite, and their backpacks and the supplies that were carried in the backpacks had proven to be priceless. Looks were definitely not important now. Survival was.

"That is where we have to go," Ryan said as he pointed to the other side of the river.

As Ryan was describing to Matthew what the next plan should be, he saw another black streak go through the water. Not again! He nudged Matthew and pointed toward where he had seen another black water beast. He didn't want to have the beast hear or see them, so he motioned for Matthew to jump to the first rock on the opposite side of the platform, toward the other side of the river they were attempting to cross.

Matthew jumped and instantly the motion attracted the water beast's attention. The ugly beast turned its head and looked right at the boys. Ryan and Matthew froze where they were, with Matthew clinging tightly to the rock and Ryan remaining on the platform. The water was whipping around them with raging speed, and they could feel their bodies trembling once again. Thankfully, the beast turned away and started moving in the opposite direction. Ryan motioned for Matthew to keep moving and Ryan did the same as he followed closely behind his best friend.

"Keep going. If we can reach the other side of the river, the beasts can't get us. We will be free and clear and we can get out of this place!" Matthew yelled as he pointed to the other side of the river while Ryan continued to jump from rock to rock behind him.

The boys knew they needed to keep jumping or they were going to be the beast's lunch and dessert. Just as the thought popped into Ryan's mind that he would definitely be the dessert portion of the meal, the water beast circled around and jumped again toward Ryan's feet. This time the beast grazed Ryan's leg with its sharp teeth.

"YEEOW! Dude! I just got bit by that beast!" Ryan yelled ahead to Matthew who was now clearing the rocks and had made it onto the other side of the riverbank.

Ryan's leg was stinging; it was excruciatingly painful. He

didn't know if he would be able to go any further, but being stranded in the middle of the raging, ice cold river with the beasts circling around him did not seem like a good alternative. As he took the next leap forward, it felt like his leg was on fire, and as he landed, it was like fireworks had exploded inside his body. He was in a tremendous amount of pain, even worse than when he landed on his butt in the pit on the prairie.

Luckily, Ryan only had one more jump to go to reach the opposite side of the riverbank, where Matthew was jumping up and down motioning for him to hurry it up. He lunged forward and landed in the snow alongside the riverbank. Ryan grabbed his wounded leg and ripped the remainder of the bottom of his pant leg off to expose the wound. He grabbed a handful of snow and pressed it against his wound, hoping to clean it and numb it up to relieve the pain.

Matthew ran over to see what Ryan was doing. He hadn't heard when Ryan had shouted across the river to tell him that he had been bitten by the water beast. Ryan took his hand off his wound and showed it to Matthew.

"Wow! That looks bad. Do you think you can walk?" Matthew asked as he watched Ryan rock back and forth in pain.

"I'm gonna have to. We need to keep going," Ryan responded as he took the pant leg he had cut off, ripped it again to increase the length, and then wrapped it around the wound.

Cold, hungry, thirsty, and now wounded, they headed off, away from the river toward a group of large pine trees that were tightly intertwined amongst one another. Matthew helped support Ryan as he hobbled alongside. As they approached the group of trees, they saw the snow had melted off all the trees and the ground. Something just wasn't quite right about this place. But, what was it?

CHAPTER 22

Matthew and Ryan continued to walk toward the wall of trees, and as they did, they could feel the warmth of the ground and the temperature starting to rise around them. They found a clearing close to the trees and took a moment to rest. Ryan's leg was still incredibly sore, and with all the excitement from the water beasts at the river, they had not offcially "received" their prizes.

The temperature had warmed up enough for them to finally take their fur coats off their shoulders, and they laid them on the ground like they were preparing for a picnic in the park. They had already slid their backpacks off their backs along with their coats, and then plopped down onto the fur blankets. It felt good not only to be on solid ground once again, but to just simply rest.

The boys dug through their backpacks to pull out their food packets and water. They discovered the extra water from the melted snow in the cave they had packed, and it started to feel like an extra special picnic lunch. As Ryan was pulling out his extra bottle of water, he felt the two keys at the bottom of his backpack and pulled those out too. He took a swig of his water and then started to examine the keys.

Ryan could not believe it when he pulled out the keys. The newest key he had taken off the platform was made of ice! Everything had moved so quickly when they were on the platform that he hadn't even noticed. It had the same etchings as the sandstone key and the same teeth pattern. The craziest thing about the ice key was that even though the temperature had warmed significantly, the key was still frozen and was not melting. He showed Matthew what he had discovered. They once again had a lot to discuss over their food packet picnic lunch.

The island games they had been playing since they arrived on the shore of the island were a true mystery. They reviewed the four quadrants they had traveled through and were amazed at themselves again as they remembered the crazy challenges they had overcome. Regardless of what was next for them, they felt they had already won the game because they had not only survived, but they were now even better friends.

The food and water went down quickly as the boys poked fun at each other. Before long, it was time for them to move again. Ryan poured a little melted snow water on his wound and wrapped it tightly again with the bottom of his pant leg.

If anyone was watching them right now, they would truly be appalled by the way the boys looked and smelled. They were absolutely filthy, and they could literally feel the dirt and grime that had accumulated on their body, in their hair, and on their clothes. Their clothes were worn and tattered, and now Ryan even had a pant leg missing. But, regardless of how they looked or smelled, they still had each other, and they had discovered along this journey they were on that was all they really needed.

"Time to move," Matthew said as he helped Ryan back to his feet once he was done wrapping his leg. The boys left the fur coats on the ground as they would be too big and heavy to take with them now that they couldn't wear them because of the heat. They stuffed their small blankets back into their backpacks, and added their empty water bottles along with the keys, then headed out for another unknown journey.

They went forward again, toward the wall of trees. At first, they thought they were back in the jungle, but quickly realized that although the climate was similar, they were definitely in a very different place. There was no going back now, so they moved on and as they did, the trees, branches, vines, and moss continued to get thicker and thicker. They were almost at the point where they could hardly push their bodies through the thickness of their surroundings. It was like they were being squeezed again as they had been in the quicksand in the desert.

Ryan and Matthew hooked arms because the last thing they wanted to have happen was for them to become separated. They felt like the defensive line of a football team pushing hard against the offensive line trying so hard to get to the quarterback. They continued to push and fight their way through the thickening of the trees and suddenly they emerged on the other side.

They could hardly believe what they were seeing. They had come out of the forest and were now staring right up the side of the towering volcano they had originally seen in the distance when they arrived on the island! They had seen the volcano from a distance from every quadrant they had been in, and now they were right on top of it. This was exactly what Ryan had envisioned when he said they needed to get up and then out of the mysterious island. He had no idea how they were going to make that happen, but he could literally feel it in his body that they were closer than they had ever been.

Straight ahead of them, they could see a river of lava flowing within a deep ravine. They also saw a rickety suspension bridge with rotting planks to walk across. Matthew and Ryan knew in order to get to the other side, they would need to cross the bridge. Then they could enter the opening they spotted along the side wall of the volcano.

As the boys stepped across the bridge, it started wobbling. Although they knew it wasn't going to be stable, based on the way it looked, they didn't expect it to be quite as rickety as it was.

"Ah! This reminds me of the challenge in the temple," Matthew said as he started to freak out, now halfway across the old bridge.

Ryan responded with a quivering voice and said, "We need to stay calm and either walk very slowly over these rickety planks, or run like crazy."

The boys quickly looked at the lava below and knew the bridge would not hold their weight for long. Without hesitating, they started running as fast as they could to cross the bridge and reach the other side. Just as they reached the last few boards of the suspension bridge, the boards broke under their feet. They both dove for the ledge and dug their hands and fingers into the dirt terrain.

Matthew pulled himself up first and then helped Ryan up

onto the ledge. Ryan's injury had really slowed him down and in this case, almost caused him to become liquid lunch for whatever beasts might be lurking within the lava. Thanks to Matthew, again, Ryan found safety on the other side of the bridge.

Matthew and Ryan picked themselves up off the ledge of the lava ravine and took off running and hobbling to the opening they had seen on the side of the volcano. As they approached the opening, it looked like a large cave. They didn't know where it would lead, but as they discussed their strategy, they imagined themselves running through the long tunnel and emerging from the other side to the finish line of a race. They imagined all of their family and friends waiting just behind the line to congratulate them on their victorious battle – for winning the island games. And then a helicopter would swoop down and pick them up out of the heart of the volcano and take them back to wherever they came from.

"I wish!" Matthew said as Ryan finished the part about the helicopter.

Ryan looked at Matthew with frustration and said, "Well, I'm pretty sure that someone has to be looking for us by now, and when they find us, they will definitely want to celebrate. Besides, I've never ridden in a helicopter before, as far as I can remember, and I thought that might be kinda cool!"

"Well, we aren't going anywhere unless we can figure out a way to get through this tunnel, and hopefully, it will lead us to the finish line. But first, we need to figure out how to light it up, otherwise, we will never be able to find our way through the dark," Matthew responded in his practical, lecturing voice.

Ryan started to look around for a couple of large sticks and said, "I will find some huge sticks, and then we can wrap one of our blankets around the top of each of the sticks and light it up like a torch."

"It's worth a shot," Matthew responded eagerly since he did not have any other brilliant ideas at the time.

The boys again recognized the value of their blankets and the risk they were taking with burning them, but they were out of options and out of time. They needed to move forward, and the opening within the wall of the volcano was the only forward direction they could take. They gathered the sticks, wrapped the blankets around the tops of them, and tied them tightly into place. Finally, they lit them up and got ready to run through the opening they had found.

The tunnel was indeed long and tortuous, and they were thankful they had devised their plan with the torches. There were tons of disgusting bugs and creepy rodents dwelling in the tunnel, but that was the last thing that was going to stop them from reaching the finish line, as they had fondly referred to it. After what seemed like hours, the boys finally reached their destination. They stepped through the last portion of the tunnel and entered into the heart of the volcano!

CHAPTER  23

"Whoa, dude! This is so cool! If we had started out here, this game wouldn't have been so bad. I think we could live here forever. It would be like our own man cave," Ryan said as he looked around at the chamber inside the volcano.

The volcano chamber had what appeared to have been at one time a river full of lava and there were stalagmites all over the walls. They could see the lava had not been active for a long time, so it had sunk low and hardened as black as tar. There was a path that had been created from the hardened lava spanning the entire base of the volcano.

The temperature was still very hot within the heart of the volcano, even though it had been dormant for what appeared to be hundreds of years. It was as if the boys were enclosed within the center of the earth. They looked up the side of the crater walls and saw a small opening, like a skylight, directly at the center that was allowing just enough light in to illuminate the crater. The boys started sweating immediately from the heat and knew they needed to locate some water as soon as they could. There had to be another prize for them somewhere inside the volcano.

The boys traveled together around the edge of the volcano, looking high and low for a sign of some food and water. Tucked deep into a small cavern about halfway around the perimeter of the volcano, they could see something reflecting the light that was coming from the skylight of the volcano's opening. The boys rushed over to the small cavern and, sure enough, the food packets and water were waiting for them, just as they had before after conquering a challenge.

Matthew dug the food packets and water out and handed half to Ryan and said, "This might literally be our last meal as there is nowhere to go from here, so enjoy."

"Except up and out," Ryan reminded Matthew with a huge grin on his face as he ripped open the food packet and chugged down a huge gulp of his water.

As the boys finished their food, they continued to scan the rugged walls of the cavernous volcano. They stood back to back and were looking in opposite directions when suddenly both boys shouted at the exact same time.

"Do you see that?" Matthew and Ryan shouted in perfect harmony but pointed in opposite directions.

They stopped for a moment and realized they were actually looking and pointing in the opposite direction, but saw the exact same thing. Along the walls of the volcano, exactly opposite each other, were a pair of keyholes in the wall. They looked in the direction the other had been pointing and then looked back at the original set of keyholes they had initially discovered. They stood in amazement at what they saw.

Although they had absolutely no idea what the keyholes were for, they realized that throughout their entire journey, they had held the keys to their future outcome all along. There was a purpose for the keys they had carried right along with them, and now they were finally about to find out their true meaning.

The boys were so excited. They grabbed the keys out of their backpacks and quickly rushed over to the first set of keyholes that Ryan had discovered and examined them intently. Around the keyholes there was a wooden plate that had the same etchings as those of the keys. The boys had no idea what the meaning of the etchings was, but they knew they must have represented something.

Maybe they were telling a story or maybe they were just telling them which key to put in which hole, but because they couldn't translate the meaning, Ryan and Matthew decided not to waste their time looking for a hidden meaning when they had the keys right in the palms of their hands. They simply had to just try something to make this work and get off the island.

The mystery of this island (the challenges, the keys, and figuring out a way off the island and back to their families) was something they weren't quite sure how to solve. However, they still felt a sense of something pulling at them to keep searching to figure out the meaning behind all of this. At this point, however, the desperation they felt to get off the island outweighed the struggle they had inside of them to solve the mystery of who or what was behind all of this; maybe getting off the island would be the key to actually solving the mystery.

At this point, they simply had to focus on what was in front of them. After examining the first set of keyholes, they ran over to the keyholes Matthew had seen and then spent the next few minutes repeating the same process. They found the same wooden plate around the keyholes with the same etchings. Matthew pulled out his keys, the wooden key from the jungle and the stone key from the prairie, and inserted them into the keyholes. He looked at Ryan, who nodded in agreement without speaking a word. As Matthew turned the keys, the boys closed their eyes and braced themselves. Nothing happened.

The boys decided to try Ryan's keys, the sandstone key from the desert and the ice key from the highlands. Ryan went to grab the ice key and was amazed to find the ice key had still not melted. He had just examined it before they exited the mountain range, and although the temperature had warmed as they began to exit, the key remained intact. Since then, the ice key had been in Ryan's backpack. Now as he held it in his hand in the extreme heat of the volcano, it was still not melting. This reassured him that these keys were indeed special and would be the answer they needed to conquering the island games and getting off the island.

"This is crazy. How did that thing not melt? We are in the middle of a volcano," Matthew expressed with astonishment as he took the key from Ryan and stared at it as if in a trance.

"Don't know. It's just another one of the mysteries of this crazy island. What I do know though is these keys have to be our answer to getting off this island," Ryan said as he took his ice key back from Matthew.

The boys continued to try combination after combination of the keys into each of the key holes, but nothing worked. They felt they had exhausted all of their options, and they were entirely exhausted themselves from the long journey they had been on and from the heat within the volcano. The boys let out a huge sigh of frustration. With their backs pressed against the wall of the volcano, they slid down the cavernous wall and landed on their butts with a thump, defeated.

"We have tried every combination of keys and nothing is working. I can't believe this. I thought for sure we had this thing figured out and it was our ticket to the helicopter ride out of here. I was waiting for the balloons and the celebration, and what did we get? Nothing! Not even a loud noise to scare us or something to indicate we might be onto something like all the times before," Ryan groaned with frustration as he put his head on his knees and ran his hands through his sticky hair.

Matthew was just as frustrated, but remained calm and said, "What are we missing, Ryan? Let's think back. Every time we captured one of these keys, we had just completed a challenge. And, every time we completed a challenge, we had to complete the challenge together...That's it! We have to do this together! It's not about the individual keys or the perfect combination. It's about putting your keys in the keyhole I found and putting my keys in the keyholes you found. We are a team, and we have to turn them all at the same time together," Matthew said as he stood up and jumped high into the air like a high school cheerleader.

"Yeah, team, yeah!" Ryan said sarcastically as he stood up and jumped as far into the air as he could with his wounded leg, trying to mock Matthew by pretending to be a cheerleader.

Matthew withdrew his excitement for a moment, rolled his eyes at his friend, and said, "Really? I just gave you the solution to what I believe will save us from this island. Better yet, will save me from having to look at your ugly hair again tomorrow morning, and that's all you have to say is yeah?"

"I just wanted to celebrate with my cheerleader friend. That's all," Ryan said sarcastically again and gave his buddy a wink and a grin.

He recognized he had gone too far this time as they were in a very serious situation and he needed to apologize, so he looked back at Matthew and said, "Sorry, man. I really was just kidding. You came up with another brilliant plan; I'm all in. Let's do it!"

With Ryan's approval, Matthew ran over to the keyholes Ryan had discovered, and Ryan waited until Matthew was in position. Once both boys were in position, they each gently took their keys and placed them into all four key holes. Nothing happened.

Ryan hollered from across the volcano, "On the count of three, we will both turn the keys together."

Matthew gave Ryan the thumbs up and Ryan began the countdown. As he shouted the number three from across the volcano, the best friends each turned their set of keys and they heard a loud click followed by a loud bang! The boys covered their ears and ran back along the edge of the volcano to meet back in the middle between the two sets of keyholes. As the boys met in the middle, they felt a sense of relief. They were finally going to make it out of there and be back home with their parents!

Suddenly the bang turned into a rumbling noise, and the boys both turned to look toward the center of the volcano. From the very heart of the volcano, the ground began to shift and lava began to rise out of the ground. The boys trembled with fear as they knew the volcano was preparing to erupt and they thought they would never make it out alive.

But just then, rising from the lava was a circular silver platform. Surprisingly, despite the heat of the lava, it wasn't melting! The boys looked at each other and turned toward the platform. They knew exactly what they needed to do.

They took a running jump and landed together onto the center of the platform. Lava was bubbling up all around them, and the temperature was climbing dramatically. Sitting in the center of the circular platform as they had done so many times before, they looked up and the light shining through the opening of the volcano was so bright they had to shield their eyes. They could tell they were still too far away from the opening of the volcano to safely escape.

The heat started to overtake them. They could feel the platform rising, but they didn't think it was fast enough to get them out of the opening of the volcano before the volcano erupted. As the pressure continued to build and the temperature continued to climb, they sat there and looked at each other with both fear and excitement.

So many times before while playing the island games, they had experienced the unknown, stepped past the fear, and remained centered in the challenge. The result had always been the blessing of another opportunity to face yet another challenge, to learn and to grow from the experience of the game.

They knew now that no matter what the outcome was of this challenge they faced to escape the heart of the volcano, they had finally conquered the island games and the mystery of the four quadrants!

The platform rose, the temperature climbed, the pressure continued to build, and then…everything went black…

MESSAGE FROM THE AUTHOR

Wow! So what do you suppose happens to Matthew and Ryan? If we consider the journey Matthew and Ryan were on, playing the island games and trying to solve the mystery of the four quadrants, we can better understand the island games are really a metaphor for the game of life we play every day. We were placed on this earth by a higher power, and each of us faces challenges routinely in our lives. It's how we show up in those challenges and what we learn from the opportunities that come our way that will define who we become as individuals and together as a team, community, and even as a society.

I have learned from my parents and my own experiences that regardless of age or circumstance, we all have a responsibility to learn and grow from the opportunities presented to us so we can become stronger individually and together. Along the way, the challenges we face may not seem fair or even reasonable at times, but perseverance to overcome and face the challenges by remaining present is the key to finding peace and remaining centered in the eye of the storm.

Although this book ends with yet another mystery about the

outcome for the boys, it's really a reflection of the fact that we truly don't know what is going to happen in our own lives; tomorrow, next month, next year, or whenever. However, we learn so many things from the adventure Matthew and Ryan were on that we can apply to our own lives.

We must appreciate what has been given to us and continue to find creative ways to expand our resources to give back to others. Everything that happens in our lives is there to serve us. Always move forward and rely not only on ourselves, but also on the support of others to overcome any obstacle. Accept the challenge and recognize that fear will always exist, but we must be willing to take the first step and focus on the goal. Live life to the fullest and play the game full out because we don't know what tomorrow will bring.

As the platform is rising, the temperature is climbing, and the pressure is building, how will you create the next chapter of your life?

Thank you for coming along on this journey of the *Island Games: Mystery of the Four Quadrants* with Matthew and Ryan, and for sharing this adventure with those you love so we can all learn and grow together. My prayer is that whatever journey you are on and whatever opportunities come along the way, you will face those challenges with renewed energy and excitement and wake up to a new adventure every day!

P.S. - If you loved this book, please post a review on Amazon by going to www.IslandGamesBook.com/review

SECRET OF THE ISLAND REVEALED...

Remember when Matthew and Ryan both dreamed of being in the lab?

Discover the Island Games adventure that even Matthew and Ryan don't remember. You can get your exclusive content **for free**, by signing up at: www.IslandGamesBook.com/secret

ABOUT THE AUTHOR

Caleb J. Boyer is an Award Winning #1 International Bestselling Author. He has been featured on ABC, NBC, CBS, FOX, and in Times Square. At twelve years old, he wrote his first full-length novel, *Island Games*, an adventure story about two best friends who,  with no memories of their past, must survive the challenges the mysterious island throws at them.

Caleb was born in Fargo, North Dakota. He became an avid reader at the very young age of four after a family tragedy had him traveling hours every day for several years. To fill the time, Caleb read every book he could get his hands on, and as a result, he developed speed reading skills so that he could read even more books. His passion for books grew to the point where he started creating his own stories. By the age of ten, he wanted to write a book in which he could incorporate the things the other books had not been able to give him. The result was the first in a series of adventure books, *Island Games.*

Caleb founded Read-Write, LLC, a company dedicated to instilling youth around the world with a passion for reading, writing, and entrepreneurship. The non-profit division of Read-Write, LLC donates books to children's hospitals so that children can have adventurous escapes as they are working to overcome their own challenges and obstacles related to their medical conditions.

Caleb has learned through life circumstances that challenges and obstacles will always exist, but favor and blessings come when you persevere through those challenges and find the strength to support, and be supported by, others.

He lives in Moorhead, Minnesota with his family.

11-18

DISCARD